Caffeine Nights Publishing

Glory Boys

Jim Iron & John Steel

Fiction aimed at the heart
and the head..

Published by Caffeine Nights Publishing 2016

CONDITIONS OF SALE

Published in Great Britain by
Caffeine Nights Publishing
4 Eton Close
Walderslade
Chatham
Kent
ME5 9AT
www. caffeinenights com

Also available as an eBook

British Library Cataloguing in Publication Data.
A CIP catalogue record for this book is available from the British Library

ISBN: 978-1-910720-47-9

Cover design by
Mark (Wills) Williams

Everything else by
Default, Luck and Accident

The authors would like to dedicate this book to Mods and Scooterists all over the world, Richard Allen, Street Sounds and all youth cults everywhere. Stay sharp.

Glory Boys

Chapter One

Friday 17th August, 1979

The service lift stunk of farts and old men's BO, and Chris Davis puffed heavily on his roll-up in an attempt to mask the stench. After what seemed like an age, the light for the 26th floor flashed up and with a dull ping the doors creaked open. Thank fuck for that, he thought as he pushed the heavy mail trolley out into the corridor. Chris threw the dog-end behind him and brushed some tiny flecks of tobacco off his arm. This was the top deck, the executive level; he had to look his best – not to suck up to these snobby bastards but just to show them how a good suit should be worn. Even at work he was immaculate, his camel-hair whistle from Johnson's was barely out of the box and his button-down shirt was so crisp it was scraping a line across the back of his neck. He straightened his back and pushed the trolley through the swing doors into the light.

Chris had been working at the Shell Centre since he had left school. He did not have many qualifications beyond O level woodwork but his sharp appearance and self-confidence had got him through the door. It was not a bad job in the mail room, overtime was plentiful and he needed plenty to fund his taste in schmutter and keep his Vespa PX in good nick. Going out was another expense and in the past six months there were clubs popping up all over town and something meaningful happening almost every night. His old Mum used to complain that he never left his bedroom and now she was bending his ear that he was never at home. The truth was that since becoming a Mod, there were far better things to do than stay in at night 'Barclaying' over old copies of Fiesta. He had to be out and see what was about. Every night at home was a missed opportunity, and he hated that dull thud of disappointment he felt when his mates recounted any eventful evening that he had missed. The job was a necessary evil and although he spent a good part of the day in the bowels of the building, delivering the mail took him all over the towering office block giving him time to catch breath-taking views of the Thames and get an eyeful of the some of the tasty crumpet that populated the building. Grown up women in stockings who smelt like the perfume stall in a posh department store...all out of his league. For now. But not forever.

The bright August sun glared through the huge windows of the top floor and even from the corridor he could catch glimpses of the whole of the city spread out around him. His city. London.

As he approached the floor's main reception, Chris felt a familiar twinge in his trousers. Lurking behind a large oak desk was Maureen Philips, a thirty-something brass with breasts like a dead heat in a Zeppelin race

'Morning Christopher,' she purred as she looked straight into his eyes. 'Have you got a package for me?'

Her tone was pure Carry On, and she had used that line endlessly but it still gave Chris a jolt to his John Thomas. He breathed in quietly and attempted to compose himself. He didn't want to appear flustered by her saucy inflection.

'Yes, I have Maureen,' he said with a smile and as he handed over a bundle of letters his eyes were drawn to her heaving bosom. Some of the geezers downstairs claimed that they had heard she always chose a top two sizes too small just to showcase her outstanding assets, but Chris thought that was bollocks. Her curvy body couldn't be contained in anything, and he was sure she would look good even in a bin bag. In truth, she was not really conventionally pretty but she made the best of what she had and the clobber she wore was always part-business, part page three.

Chris heard a husky 'ahem' behind him and his attention snapped away from Maureen's glorious stackers. It was one of the executives, a tall streak of public school piss in a Savile Row suit.

The lanky nob did not even look at Chris as he spoke.

'Did that brief from Goldman's arrive, Miss Philips?'

'Yes Mister Cavendish,' piped Maureen in a clipped tone as she rustled through the mail Chris had handed over. She looked at him and delivered a curt 'That's fine, thank you' which really translated as 'You can fuck off now.' Chris sneered and pushed his trolley off with a jolt. *The tart.*

'Where the hell have you been?' roared Alec Norton as Chris pushed his empty trolley into the mailroom. Norton was the mail room manager, a bad-tempered jock who sweated like James Brown and seemed to delight in being a pain in Chris's khyber. Chris ignored him and began to reload for his next delivery.

'Hey Ted, I'm talking to you,' continued Norton.

'I'm not a Ted, I'm a Mod,' said Chris with resignation.

'Ted, Mod, whatever you are... It's all a lot of shite anyway. That was a forty-minute delivery and you've dragged it out to an hour and a half.'

'The service lift was running slow and I had to wait for a few signatures,' Chris shrugged without looking round.

'Bollocks,' barked his red-faced boss. 'You were eyeing up the birds and puffing away at those fags. You reek of Old Holborn.'

Chris said nothing and finished loading his trolley. He hated this job at times but he hated Norton more. The beer-bellied twat in the ill-fitting whistle was always on his case. They'd got off to a bad start on Chris's first day at work when Norton seemed alarmed to see this smart dressed upstart introduced to his department. The rest of the new starts were the usual teenage oiks jammed uncomfortably into ill-fitting slacks and the shirts they usually only wore to weddings and funerals. Kids whose idea of music began and ended with Judas fucking Priest or occasionally the Lurkers. But Chris was sharp and he knew it, and it seemed to make Norton massively ill at ease. The fact that Chris had been noticed and his appearance complimented on by some of Norton's superiors was also a kick to the nuts that made the sweaty Jock even more resentful.

'This next delivery should only take you half an hour so you can take these as well.' Norton threw a pile of parcels on top of Chris's trolley.

'Whoa,' exclaimed Chris as he looked at the parcels and then his watch. 'These are for the Downstream building. That's miles away. I'm finishing at two.'

'Well you had better get a fucking move on then,' the Scotsman sneered with a grin.

Chris was about to retort but he held back. Over an hour's work to do and only half an hour left on his shift. He pushed the trolley determinedly through the swing doors. He would do it with time to spare so fuck Norton, fuck Shell and fuck Maureen Philips's enormous knockers. The weekend was almost here and his real life was about to begin.

***

By the time Chris got to the car park, work was a distant memory. It was a talent he had perfected over the few years he had been there. As soon as he kicked his scooter into life and tore out of the main gate his repetitive daily grind, Norton and all the other two-bob cunts were forgotten as his mind raced with the possibilities that lay before him. Getting together with his mates, shopping for clothes and music, getting pilled up and pulling a renee. More important than all that it was the feeling of being something. Being a Mod, to be *someone*. Someone different, smarter, BETTER.

At work he was just another cog in the wheel among all the straights and old bastards that thought a couple of pints at the weekend and a two-minute pump on their bored wife was all life had to offer. It was only when he was not working that he really felt alive.

Chris hit the rush hour traffic with abandon, and cut his way across the city back to Canning Town using every short cut and rat run he knew. Before he got home he made his way down to Selman's Records to pick up something he had been waiting for all week. The old geezer that ran the shop was a miserable cowson but it was close to home and he was fairly good at ordering anything beyond the standard chart fare he usually flogged. When he entered the shop it was empty and there was a bit of Matt Munro warbling over the ancient speakers behind the counter.

The Impossible Dream. None of Chris's dreams felt impossible. The future was there to be written.

The owner shuffled through from the back shop as if serving customers was a massive draw on his resources. 'Yes?' he said bluntly.

'I ordered a record last week,' said Chris. 'Secret Affair?'

'Never bleedin' heard of them. A new band is it? Another one of that punk rabble.'

'They're not punk,' said Chris sullenly. 'You took my name. Chris Davis.'

'Davis, Davis,' muttered the old man as he flicked through a dog-eared hardback book on the counter. 'Ah, yes. I-Spy? Hold on a minute.' He disappeared into the back shop and emerged with the single in his grasp. 'Time For Action? Why is it in a brown paper bag? It's not dirty is it? I won't sell that type of stuff here.'

'That's the one,' said Chris. His heart leapt. Buying records always gave him a buzz but this one was special. This was a band he had seen grow rapidly over the past six months, each gig better than the next. This was a band that had acknowledged him and his mates, chatted to them, drank with them even. They even had a name for their older followers: GLORY BOYS. The Mod elite.

Now Secret Affair were on vinyl at last and Chris had a copy of his own. He paid the old bastard and shot out of the shop as if he had just nicked it. He had to hear this record as soon as possible. As the bell above the door echoed around the empty shop the bloke behind the counter sneered. Another fly-by-night bunch of herberts being peddled by the record companies. He had seen it all before, there was no substitute for real class. He cranked the Matt Monro record up a few notches and retreated into the back shop. Matt was singing Yesterday now. The old cunt was living it.

Chris pulled his scooter up in the small patch of grass that passed for a garden in front of his house and immediately pulled over an old tarpaulin that he kept under the hedge. He knew it was not exactly high security but it kept the casual passer-by from ogling his wheels and it protected the chrome from the polluted drizzle that often drifted over from the nearby factories. Living in Canning Town was all Chris had ever known and he felt at home here but there were some real dodgy types around. Since the docks shut, the area had deteriorated. There were glue-sniffing boneheads on his corner, greasers in the caff and lazy work-shy bastards in the pubs who preferred getting out of their nuts and half-inching other people's hard-earned gear rather than making their own money. Scum who stole off their own rather than having the common decency to hit the posher folk up West.

He was confident that he and his mates had enough of a reputation around their patch to dissuade the casual scooter thief unless they were keen on a brick round the head and a four pairs of hush puppies booting them in the balls.

Chris leapt up the stairs to his room and was pleased to see his new suit and shirt laid out on his bed, ironed to perfection by his mum. Even his tie had been done. His parents were still at work and the house was deadly quiet but not for long. He slapped on the Secret Affair single and cranked it up. His tinny music centre did its best to cope, and the brassy intro to Time For Action filled the room. He had never felt such a buzz from a record before, all his old 1960s records and Jam albums were great but this was happening now, right now, and he was in the middle of it. He did some shuffling around the room as the track washed over him. He was no hoofer but he did his best, especially when no one was looking. As soon as the track finished he played it again then flipped it over to the B-side. Soho Strut was another song he had heard at gigs down at the Bridge House and elsewhere. Fucking amazing. He started to get dressed. He had to get out and get the evening started. Tonight he was meeting the lads at The Wellington, and Squire were playing. He had seen them before at the Bridge. He wasn't that fussed about them but they were a Mod band and sure to attract a good crowd. Hopefully they would attract a few tasty sorts as well.

Chris had his eye on someone in particular but any port in a storm would do. As long as it wasn't that little gypsy-looking boiler who had tried to give him a blow job in the park near the Barge Aground. Anything could happen, the weekend starts here. He looked at the clock, maybe there was time for a J Arthur?

Dave Hughes and Billy Keegan were waiting at the corner of Butchers Road, puffing away on roll-ups and standing beside their gleaming Lambrettas. It was just after 6 p.m. and the summer sun was just taking on a dull orange glow.

'Where the fuck is he?' said Billy.

'Probably doing his hair, the fucking old woman,' spat Dave.

'I want to get moving, what's holding him up?'

'Take it easy,' said Dave. 'What's the hurry? It's early doors yet.'

'I want to get some gear from Gaff before it's all gone.'

Dave noticed that Billy was flipping his scooter keys from hand to hand and round his fingers. 'You sure you haven't had some already?'

'Just a little,' protested Billy. 'I had a couple of blues left over from Monday at the Bridge.'

Dave sighed and flicked what was left of his oily rag end into the road.

'What?' said Billy in an annoyed tone.

'It's not even gone dark and you are speeding out of your tits already. We've got the whole weekend ahead.'

'Yeah?' said Billy, 'And I ain't going to see the back of my eyelids until Monday morning. What's wrong with that, Mary Whitehouse?'

There was a familiar sound of a rattling Vespa approaching as Chris appeared round the corner and pulled his scooter to halt beside them.

'Hey, hey, here he is,' shouted Billy over the din.

Chris turned his engine off and pulled the scooter on to its stand.

'Where the fuck have you been?' said Dave.

'I had a few things to finish off.'

'I told you,' Billy said to Dave. 'Wanking again. He can't keep his hands off it.'

Dave laughed and Chris looked angry. Annoyed that he had been rumbled and annoyed knowing that he should have laughed it off.

Dave put a condescending hand on Chris's shoulder.

'You do know it's not true that if you beat your meat before shagging a bird you'll last longer.'

Billy roared with laughter.

'Yes, you'll still be done at two pumps and a shiver.'

'Fuck off,' said Chris. He had wanted to deliver a wittier, more of an Oscar Wild-type response, but he couldn't think of anything and just wanted the piss-taking dead in its tracks. 'Are we going to the Wellington or what?'

'Yeah, yeah,' said Dave. 'Just wait till I roll an oily.'

As Dave reached into the deep front pocket of his parka there was a muffled clunk.

'What you got in there?' said Billy, 'Yer mum's chastity belt?'

'No, this,' said Dave as he pulled a claw hammer out. 'Now shut it about my old dear or I'll knock your teeth out.'

Chris felt a quick jolt of unease. Dave had a dry wit but he was never quite sure when he meant business. He had a notorious reputation at school and down at West Ham, and although he had embraced the Mod scene, Dave had a history of tear-ups with punters from all over London and wherever they went he was never truly relaxed. His home life was a mess as well and, while he was a good friend, he often dragged them into confrontations that could have been avoided.

'Why have you brought that with you?' asked Chris.

'For repairs and that,' said Dave unconvincingly.

'What are you going to repair?' said Billy. 'Some rocker's skull? You are a fucking nut job. Just like your old man.'

Dave dropped the hammer as he leapt across the path and grabbed Billy by the neck, pushing him up against his scooter. The GP125 rocked on its stand but did not fall.

'Watch me fucking scooter,' yelled Billy but he could see from Dave's eyes that that was the least of his worries.

'You mention my old man again and they will be scraping your canister off the pavement,' spat Dave.

Chris laid a hand on Dave's shoulder.

'Dave, he didn't mean it. Calm down mate.' Dave turned and stared at him with such fury that Chris thought he was going to get it next but then Dave slowly relaxed his grip on Billy.

'Yeah, I was only joking,' said Billy attempting to regain his composure. 'Don't take everything so serious you...' Billy realised what he was about to say and let his words drift off into the atmosphere.

Dave grabbed his helmet off the saddle of his scooter.

'All right then, let's fucking go.' He jammed on his helmet, gave his kick-start a furious dig and set off into the traffic.

Billy and Dave looked at each other as they got ready to follow him.

'Should be an eventful night,' said Billy with a giggle.

Chris was not so sure.

***

Chris was buzzing with excitement. He liked The Wellington and had always had a good time there. It was an odd boozer and it sat on Waterloo Road jammed so close to the railway that the building rumbled at regular intervals as trains passed by. Upstairs it was cut in two by another railway line from Waterloo East so sometimes a quiet drink in there was like supping a pint during the Blitz. It was not the most glamorous of battle-cruisers and was mostly populated by the dossers that seem to be attracted to train stations. The Merton Parkas had something of a residency there, The Purple Hearts and The Chords had played as well so it had gradually been adopted by the growing Mod population around London. It always attracted a lot of good-looking Mod girls and Chris had seen one sort in particular who really tickled his fancy. He had always bottled out of speaking to her before but maybe tonight was the night. A little 'chemical confidence' from his mate Gaff and he would be in there like Flynn.

Billy, Chris and Dave parked their scooters up round the corner of the pub alongside a fair few others that were already in place.

'Looks like a busy one tonight,' said Dave.

'Can't think why for fucking Squire,' said Billy as he packed his gloves into his helmet and straightened out his parka.

'They are all right,' said Chris. 'It will be a good night anyway. Especially once we've seen Gaff.'

Dave scowled at Chris.

'Yeah, if he has any gear left. We would have been here ages ago if you weren't poofing about with your hair.'

'And wanking,' laughed Billy.

Chris said nothing and walked towards the pub.

Inside The Wellington, the band was in full flow and sweat was already starting to drip off the roof. Bodies were packed together right up to the tiny raised area that passed for a stage. At the front it was just possible to notice the dividing line between band and punters. As he walked through the door with Billy and Dave, Chris felt a real rush of excitement. The room was packed with Mods, apart from a few resident winos in the corner, and the atmosphere was buzzing. This was what it was all about for Chris, all Mods together with most of the squares and mugs locked outside. He scanned the crowd and saw a lot of familiar faces and a good few new ones too. The scene seemed to be growing every week, something good was happening and he was right at the heart of it. He reached into his parka pocket and pulled out his camera. It was a small compact job but it was an original 1960s Kodak Brownie 44A that his Grandad had given him not long before he died. Chris carried it with him most of the time and loved to capture the moment when he was out at a club or with his mates. Looking back at his pictures always gave him a proper buzz and he already had small library of photos from the Mod scene.

'Stop checking out the birds you twat and get the beers in.' Dave thumped Chris in the back and broke him out of his daydream.

'Fuck the beers,' said Billy scanning the room. 'Where's Gaff?'

It was never hard to find Gary 'Gaff' Arthur because he always had a crowd around him. Although he was quite small he had a big personality. Maybe that's what attracted people to him or maybe it was because he was a notorious speed dealer. Gaff was not your usual drug peddler, for him, speed was just a best seller amongst all his many other enterprises. It was simple supply and demand, if punters at the clubs had wanted fucking clackers he would have sold them instead. But uppers were what the kids wanted and he felt it was his duty to help them out. If he made a bit of cash while doing it then so be it. He needed the pretty green same as anyone and raking through Oxfam for original 1960s suits was not for him. All his gear was made to measure and it was not cheap, plus he liked holding folding; it felt good to have a bit of cash to spread around and the birds seemed to enjoy it. You'd be surprised how many of the Richards who'd taken whizz off him 'on account' had repaid his bellend with a good polish.

Chris had been friends with Gaff since secondary school and they had always been good mates. Billy and Dave had been a few years above them and very rarely made an appearance anyway. When Chris first got a sniff of the Mod scene, Gaff had been initially unimpressed and more focused on his many entrepreneurial interests most of which focused on selling on hooky gear whenever possible. Chris continued to drag Gaff along to gigs and gradually he came round. Once he found out there was a gap in the market flogging speed though, he was in with the bricks – suits, scooter and haircut all within a couple of weeks.

Dave noticed Gaff holding court close to the gent's bogs.

'Gaff', he yelled. 'Over here'.

Gaff waved and carried on dealing with his regulars.

Dave wasn't having that, he glared and yelled his instruction once again.

Gaff shook off his hangers-on and snaked his way through the crowd.

'All right geezers? What kept you?' he said.

'We had to wait on Davis,' said Billy. 'He was at home beating himself blind.'

'What?' said Gaff, unsure of whether this was a piss-take at his expense.

'Fuck off,' said Chris. 'You don't get to look this good without a bit of graft. You're looking pretty sharp as well Gaff. Is that a new whistle?'

Before Gaff could answer Dave butted in, 'Never mind all that old pony. Have you got any gear left?' He motioned over to the small gathering Gaff had left behind. 'I hope you haven't flogged it all to them dozy pricks.'

'Don't you worry Mr Hughes, I've got a selection of my finest wares right here. Usual price of course but it's the good stuff.' Gaff handed his mates a small bag of blue pills each and held out his hand for remuneration.

Dave jabbed some crumpled notes into his palm. 'They had better be good, not the usual shit you get from that fucking Ted.'

Gaff's main supplier was a hairy-arsed Rockabilly from Custom House. He knew his mates did not like him fraternising with 'grease' but Gaff liked the guy and he wasn't about to let sub-cultural divides get in the way of good business.

'Of course not,' he lied. 'This is good gear. New supplier.'

'Cheers mate, back in a minute,' said Billy as he headed straight for the bogs.

Gaff also made his excuses and left to continue his one-man pharmaceutical sales drive leaving Chris standing next to Dave who was scowling and scanning the room silently. Chris felt that initial buzz fading as he stood next to his sullen mate and listened to the band but his heart leapt once more when he caught sight of what he had been hoping for. Over near the bottom end of the bar was a gorgeous 2-Tone bird laughing and joking with a couple of her ugly mates. He had seen her before in The Wellington and down at the Bridge but never quite plucked up the guts to chat her up. Tonight she was looking better than ever with her hot shapely figure squeezed into a black Fred Perry and tonic mini skirt. She had the full package – feather cut, fishnets, white ankle socks and shiny Doc Marten shoes. Chris felt his loins stir, he had to make a move. He tipped a few of the blues into his hand, necked the lot and then gulped down what remained of his pint. Time for action.

Charlotte Timms was just reaching the climax of telling a particularly dirty joke as Chris wandered over. Her friends were cackling like witches and Chris stood at the edge of the group awkwardly waiting for the hilarity to die down. Charlotte looked at him and raised her eyebrows a little, indicating that she was waiting for him to say something.

'I, eh, I was wondering if I could take your photo,' he mumbled.

'Eh? Who are you? Fucking David Bailey,' said Charlotte and her friends started to giggle again.

Chris was taken aback by her sharp tongue but now that he was close to her he could see that she was even more beautiful than he had thought so he stumbled on.

'No, I... eh, just like taking snaps of the, eh... Mod scene.'

'Oh all right then,' she said with a wicked smile. 'Snap on then, eh... whatever your name is?'

'It's Chris. Chris Davis.'

'All right then Chris Davis,' she said with a sarcastic tone. 'I'm Charlotte Timms and this is Barbara and Jill now get to a fucking move on then, we ain't got all night.'

Chris lifted up his camera and got Charlotte in his sights from head to toe.

'Hold up,' she protested, 'It's not just me in the frame is it? What about Barbara and Jill?'

'Of course,' he said as he stepped back a little to fit the two boilers in as well. Where would Cinderella be without her sisters?

The flashbulb popped and Chris moved in again slightly to get a solo shot of Charlotte before she could protest. Flash, bang, wallop and he knew he had the smudge he wanted. Gorgeous.

'That's a nice camera. Very retro,' said Charlotte and she moved a little closer to Chris, just out of orbit of her two friends who were now focusing on Squire as they announced their final song of the night.

'Yeah, it was my grandad's. It's just a hobby,' he mumbled.

'All right. So what other hobbies do you have Chris,' she said with a mischievous glint in her eye that both unsettled Chris and turned him on.

'Scooter, clothes, bands... all the Mod stuff,' mumbled Chris. 'That takes up most of my time outside of work. What about you?'

'I like a lot of sixties music but some of these new bands are a bit rough,' said Charlotte. 'It's just punks in Fred Perrys.'

Chris bit his lip. That was not what he believed but he did not want to have a straight up argument with her at this stage.

'I take it you're into Ska?' said Chris.

'Yeah, Ska, bluebeat, rocksteady, some of the new 2-Tone stuff. That's always interested me more. There's so much more stuff out there.'

Chris immediately thought of a bit of a line, paused for a moment as it was a bit cheesy, then used it anyway.

'Sounds good, maybe you could give me a bit of an education in it.'

Charlotte frowned a bit and Chris felt his heart sink then she giggled slightly.

'Maybe I could. There's a cracking Ska night at the Ace every Wednesday. Maybe you could come along.'

Chris tried to sound cool, calm and collected but it did not work. 'That sounds great,' he blurted out. 'Yeah, definitely.'

Charlotte seemed to giggle a little at his eagerness as she reached into her bag for an eyebrow pencil.

'Have you got a bit of paper?'

Chris fumbled in his parka pocket and pulled out a photocopied flyer for a Mod club down in Southall.

'Here, use this.'

Charlotte rested the scrap of paper on Chris chest and etched out her number on it.

'There you go. If ever you fancy a real Ska night out away from these herberts just give me a call.'

'I will, yeah,' said Chris then he dried up.

'All right then,' said Charlotte as she turned back to her friends, 'See ya.'

Chris wandered back to the bar with the paper tightly in his grip. Gaff, Billy and Dave were huddled together in conversation.

'All right, here he is, Casanova,' said Gaff as Chris approached them.

'What's happening with her?' said Billy.

'Nothing,' said Chris. 'Just talking.'

'Just talking?' Billy sneered. 'You're losing your touch.'

Gaff stepped into the centre of the group and laid a hand on Billy and Chris' chest as if he was a boxing referee.

'That's out of order now Bill. He's still got his charm. I mean he was touching your sister's fanny round at yours last week while you were in the bath.'

'Cheeky cunt,' growled Billy and pushed Gaff's hand away.

'All right, all right,' said Dave. 'Stop fucking about. What's happening? It's nearly over in here and I'm just coming up on those bombers.'

'We could go up west,' said Gaff. 'See what's happening at the Marquee. I've still got a few pills that need flogging.'

'Yeah, all right,' said Dave. 'It's better than fuck all I suppose.'

'Let's go down to the tea hut before we go,' said Billy. 'I'm fucking starving.'

They all agreed and started to walk towards the greasy spoon a few streets down, taking a stroll past were there scooters were parked to check they were all right. Just then, around the corner came the Morgan boys, a seven strong skinhead gang who had been buzzing glue under the railway arches.

The Morgans were a bunch of boneheads from the nearby Hatfield and Roupell Street estates and the area around Waterloo was regarded as their patch. Not everyone agreed but when they were full of Evo-Stik and cheap lager there would never be much discussion – only a tear-up would sort it out. Barry and Mark Morgan were twin brothers and the leading lights of the mob. These cut price Kray Twins had an old man in choky and a mother often flat on her back working out ways to pay the rent, so they had learnt to fend for themselves from an early age. They had not learned much though beyond thieving and sticking the boot in but at seventeen they had muscles and facial hair growth that would put a docker to shame. The rest were the usual mix of local louts who chose to fight with the Morgan brothers rather than be their victims, apart from one particularly nasty little shit known as Monkey Harris. Harris was not a great talent at brawling but he seemed to relish sticking the boot in after the rest had done their damage and he was overly fond of putting his blade to use when the opportunity arose.

'Oi, oi,' yelled Barry. 'It's the moped boys. Evening all.'

The Morgan twins' followers sniggered gormlessly as the skins circled around Chris, Billy and Dave.

'Nice PX,' said Mark as he stroked the Chrome mirrors on Chris's scooter. 'Pity you've covered it with all this shit.'

'Get your hands off it, bonehead,' said Chris as he immediately regretted opening his mouth.

'Get your hands off it,' parroted Mark as he looked to his mob for appreciation of his cutting wit. He got it with another round of gormless sniggers.

Dave flitted a furious gaze between the brothers but said nothing. His fingers tightened around the tool in his parka pocket.

'We're sick of you poofs hanging around here every week,' said Barry. 'The Wellington is our boozer.'

'You're banned from it anyway Morgan,' said Billy. 'Besides, they don't serve glue behind the bar.'

Barry Morgan turned purple almost immediately and his boot lashed out, kicking a wing mirror off Chris' scooter.

The clatter of chrome and broken glass was the trigger and Dave had his hammer out and swinging in an instant. He lunged towards Barry Morgan but one of the other boneheads got in the way and received a crack in the skull for his troubles. Billy leapt towards Mark and whacked his crash helmet off the hulking skinhead's shoulder. Billy and Dave had been in enough rumbles to know that making a move for the top boys first always opened up the possibility that some of their sheep would fade into the background. It was a fair idea but it was not working tonight, boots and fists rained down on Dave and Billy and Chris had two boot boys laying into him while Monkey Harris hopped around excitedly in the background looking for his opportunity to put his Stanley knife to work. Dave took another foot-soldier out the picture with his swinging hammer but the handle, now smeared in blood, slipped from his grasp. As he reached onto the pavement for his tool, Barry Morgan caught him on the chest with a steel toe-capped kick that dropped him to the ground wheezing. Billy and Mark Morgan were grappling together and they crashed into Billy's scooter sending it and them onto the tarmac with a thud. Chris was doing his best to fend off the blows but he was taking a pounding and could feel a real sting of fear that he was going to get cut up into the bargain.

The sound of Billy's scooter smashing to the ground must have alerted some of the other punters outside The Wellington as Chris heard some shouting in the background and noticed a dozen or so Mods running towards them. The Morgan boys were either too brave or too stupid to run and they stood their ground. Chris took the opportunity to punch one of his attackers in the bollocks as he pulled himself back onto his feet. Monkey Harris also took his chance and he jabbed his blade towards Chris face. He was too far away to do much damage but the tip of the knife caught Chris on the cheek.

The road was full of writhing bodies but outnumbered, the Morgans were pulling back and the punch-throwing descended into empty bravado and threats as heavy with expletives as any Jimmy Jones stag show. Before Chris could even touch his cheek to assess the damage, Monkey Harris was off on his toes. Billy helped Dave back to his feet but Dave shrugged off his assistance and picked up his hammer.

'Are you all right mate?' asked Billy but Dave remained silent, gripping his blood-stained tool and glaring at the retreating skins. As they pulled themselves back together and got Billy's GP back on its stand, Chris noticed Charlotte leaving the Wellington with her friend. A few Mod girls had made their way over to see what the disturbance was and revel in the drama but Charlotte looked disinterested, disgusted even, and walked on. That's fucking great thought Chris and he felt a dull thud in his stomach that hurt more than the throb on his jaw from that knuckle sandwich delivered by one of the Morgan boys. Now she probably thought he was just one of the cavemen trading blows with the mugs on the cobbles. As he watched her go he crumpled the piece of paper with her phone number on it and hurled it into the gutter. It was no good to him now.

'Chris. Chris,' Gaff's voice grew stronger in the background.

'What?' said Chris angrily as he stirred from his foul mood.

'Put your knob back in and let's go,' laughed Gaff.

'What are you talking about?'

'Look at your strides mate,' roared Billy.

Chris looked down and noticed that his suit trousers were split from the waist to the crotch. Sticking the boot into one of the Morgan boys felt satisfying but his zip was bust wide open and his clean, white under-crackers were clearly visible.

'For fuck's sake,' he gasped.

The rest of the lads were pissing themselves laughing and the sting of fresh cuts and bruises were long forgotten.

'Come on Davis,' smirked Dave. 'Get your balls back in and let's go. The night ain't over yet.'

Chapter Two

Chris, Billy and Dave were standing outside Canning Town tube station silently. The Saturday morning rush was all around them as the locals tried to make the most out of their 48-hour reprieve from the dull numbness of the working week. All three of them were smart but casually dressed and they all bore the cuts and bruises from the previous night's fracas with the Morgan morons outside the Wellington. Billy and Dave were puffing furiously on their cancer sticks and staring into the distance; Chris was visibly uneasy although he tried to hide it.

'Where the fuck is Gaff?' said Dave for the third time through gritted teeth. 'He'd better not make us late for this. We'll look like right mugs if we are not there for the train.'

'He'll be here. Don't panic,' said Billy.

'We're not fucking about today,' Dave continued. 'These are the top boys. I told them we would be there.'

'All right, all right,' said Billy. 'It's just some fucking hooligans we are meeting up with, not the Masons.'

Dave threw his fag end onto the street and ground it into the pavement with his foot.

'It's the ICF. Not some fucking scarf-waving dickheads. It's a chance for us to be part of something bigger.'

Chris finally snapped out of his silent contemplation.

'Is this what we want, is it? Trading blows with every herbert up and down the second division every weekend?'

'Why? You got something better to do?' challenged Dave.

'Yes, what about gigs and scooter runs to the coast. There is Mod stuff happening all the time now. We don't want to miss that. Do we?'

'We can do that anytime,' Dave said witheringly. 'This is what it's all about.'

Chris did not agree but kept his mouth shut. To him the Mod scene was everything –the clothes, the bands, the scooters and the like-minded people. It was a full-time package. The thought of rolling around the cobbles every weekend with a bunch of yobs filled him with despair. Still, Billy and Dave seemed excited by it so he felt he had to oblige. It would probably just descend to a lot of shouting and running at each other with the Old Bill in the middle anyway.

'Here he is,' said Billy pointing at Gaff's figure in the distance.

Gaff approached the trio clutching a large plastic bag.

'All right chaps,' he said with a grin.

'Where the fuck have you been?' snapped Dave.

'And good morning to you too Mr Hughes,' Gaff said with a laugh.

'I told you. Ten on the dot.'

'Jah wohl mein commandant,' snapped Gaff still smiling. 'I had to pick up some gear. I don't want to let go of a good opportunity to move some merchandise.'

'What's in the bag,' said Dave. 'Have you brought your packed lunch with you?'

'Very funny Davey boy,' said Gaff as he reached into his bag. 'These are the finest leisure shirts available. Three button, short sleeves and Italian design.' He pulled a lurid polyester top out and gave the guys a closer look.

'That's fucking horrible,' said Billy. 'You wouldn't get me near that.'

'And you wouldn't get me near a lighted match with that,' joked Chris. 'Come on Gaff, who is going to buy that? These are the type of thing my grandad wears. The static off them things could shock a corpse back to life.'

'How dare you,' said Gaff in mock outrage. 'These are what the best dressed terrace terrors are wearing in every top firm... as far as the Welsh know anyway.'

'We are going to Wrexham to kick the shit out of them,' said Dave. 'Not to flog them moody clobber.'

'No reason we can't do both, Mr Hughes,' said Gaff. 'No reason at all. These will sell like hotcakes mate. They had fucking better, I've got fifteen of them in here. I got them off an Indian geezer in Shepherd's Bush.'

Chris was getting tense and tiring of the small talk.

'Look, if we are going to go, let's fucking go,' he said and made his way into the underground. Dave set after him quickly, desperate to make sure it was him that was leading the charge. Billy and Gaff raised their eyebrows at each other and followed behind.

As they emerged from the underground at Euston station the atmosphere was electric. Every Saturday was the same, little pockets of firms meeting up for their own away day adventure and eyeing each other warily. The temptation for a pre-match punch-up was always there but getting to the game was more important (unless they were Millwall). Rival London firms could get a kicking any day of the week but the opportunity to travel beyond the M25 and take a boot at some provincial shit-kickers was the main goal.

Dave noticed a small gathering of Mods and terrace terrors across the concourse and he gestured for his mates to follow him. Chris and Billy got the message but Gaff was already laying some spiel on a group of scarfers and attempting to flog them his shady sports tops. Chris recognised the other Mods almost immediately. They were the Glory Boys, an older group of mainly ex-skins from around Becontree and Barking. They looked smart as fuck but Chris knew they had a reputation for violence. They followed Secret Affair around the country and had caused a near riot at a gig up in Sheffield fairly recently then someone got battered with a hammer at another concert in Canterbury. Maybe that was the inspiration behind Dave's weapon of choice? Chris felt uneasy. This trip to Wales could get out of hand very easily.

'Who the fuck are they?' said Mickey Thomson, one of the larger Glory Boys as he waved a dismissive finger between Chris and Billy.

'Good mates of mine,' said Dave. 'They're all right.'

'They'd fucking better be,' said Mickey. 'We don't want no runners today. If any cunt has it off on his toes today I'll fucking do them myself.'

Chris felt a bolt of panic as he realised that he would definitely be seeing some active service. Better to take a kicking from some anonymous sheep-shaggers and be done with it rather than have the Glory Boys on his trail back home. Another of the older Mods, Terry Harkins, leaned into the conversation.

'Is this it then? The Canning Town mob.' he sneered. 'Three geezers?'

'And my mate Gaff over there,' said Dave.

'I know that little cunt,' Terry continued. 'Is he dealing today?'

'A few pills, Yeah,' said Billy with a hint of antagonism.

'Well you tell him to dump them if he gets pulled by the OB. We don't want any cunt saying the ICF are a bunch of fucking junkies.'

Dave nodded fairly meekly. Chris was a little shocked at how reverent Dave seemed to be to these guys. Maybe he knew something he didn't. Chris had seen the blokes at the Barge Aground and the Bridge more than a few times and, while they seemed to be well respected amongst other Mods, surely they were not all that? Were they?

A shout went out that the train was in and they all started to move as one towards the platform.

'C'mon Gaff, for fuck's sake,' yelled Dave.

Gaff was still on the main concourse flogging his remaining clobber to what looked like a couple of European backpackers. Chris sniggered as he was sure that it was unlikely that his mate was giving them the fairest rate of exchange. Gaff approached them with an exaggerated hand-rubbing gesture signalling that his shady wares had been a sell out.

'Did you do well then?' asked Chris.

'Very well Chrissy boy, I'm a bit disappointed there is nothing left for the Welsh boys.'

'All they will be getting from me is a boot in the balls,' mumbled Dave. 'Come on, let's get a fucking move on.'

Dave stormed on ahead with Billy close behind him and Chris and Gaff followed.

The train to Chester was the worst that British Rail could muster from its dilapidated rolling stock. It was the usual football special that came pre-wrecked with cracked windows, ripped seating and a bog already overflowing with shit. Everyone piled on and Dave dragged the lads forward to make sure that they all got as close as possible to the Glory Boys and their associates. The journey was pretty uneventful apart from a bit of argy-bargy at Chester station with some local football fans who were on their way to some low-rent third division tie. Things got a bit quieter on the final leg of the journey as the anticipation grew and the train trundled closer to the Welsh border town where the Wrexham Frontline undoubtedly waited for their English counterparts.

Chris sat silently, peering out of the window at the grey borderland countryside. How could even the fields have so little colour about them? Maybe it really was 'grim up north' and what the fuck was he doing here on a Saturday afternoon when he could have been window-shopping in Savile Row or cruising around town for some new parts for his PX? He might even have seen Charlotte about. Maybe she hadn't seen him rolling around in the street with those Morgan mugs and there was still a chance. Probably not though, as he was bound to pick up a few new knocks and bruises today. Thirty London yobs nipping over the border for a punch-up were bound to be noticed. Not one of them had a single scarf or badge to show that they were West Ham but as soon as they hit town they would be marked men. None of them were wearing wellingtons for a start, a dead giveaway to the Wrexham hillbillies.

'Here, hold this,' said Gaff as he thrust a desert boot into Chris's hand, rousing him from his daydream.

'What,' said Chris hazily. 'What the fuck are you doing?'

Gaff was jamming a wad of pound notes and fivers into his sock under the arch of his foot.

'I've sold all those bombers. This lot are popping them like Smarties. I don't want them Welsh muppets getting their mitts on this bundle.'

'So it's safe down there is it?' Chris said sarcastically.

'It is unless they strip me down. These bleedin' Taffs like to do a bit of taxing if they've got you spark out on the pavement.

'Great weekend,' said Chris moodily. 'Beaten and stripped by a bunch of woolly-backs.'

'You're a good looking chap Chrissy boy,' laughed Gaff. 'I'm sure they will treat you gently.' He laughed again. 'You won't be able to sit down for a week.'

Gaff noticed that Chris was silent and he stopped giggling. He knew his mate did not really expect to get bummed by the Welsh but he could tell he was uneasy about the whole away day.

'Look mate,' he said quietly, 'We will be all right. When the Taffs see us coming they will be off on their toes. We are with the famous ICF and we're West Ham. We practically invented football hooliganism. It's our gift to the world.'

Chris smiled a little.

'That's more like it,' said Gaff. 'Now give me that fucking shoe back, I think we are here.'

Before the train had even stopped one of the ICF stood up and began barking orders. He was not Mod but he had a short barnet and was smartly dressed in Levis, a Ben Sherman and a Harrington.

'Here we are lads. Stick together and we will roll right through these fucking Taffs.'

There was a cacophony of rowdy yelling and everyone was on their feet ready to pile out of the carriage doors onto foreign soil. As they hit the platform the sky was overcast and foreboding. Dave's eyes were gleaming as he and Billy pushed their way to the front.

'Gaff. Chris. Stick with us,' he yelled back.

Despite their lively exit from the train their journey to Wrexham's Racecourse ground was uneventful and a full-on tear up with the frontline never materialised. Even inside the ground there was little antagonism directed towards them even though the ICF led a vocal assault that left no doubt that they were present. Chris was looking around the stadium in a detached way, not really paying much attention to the action on the pitch. His group stuck out like a sore thumb in the Kop End, surrounded by a sea of scarf waving Hammers. A sea was probably a generous description as it was closer to a pond. Even for this early in the season the London turnout was poor. The Wrexham punters were not exactly filling the ground to capacity either. Chris looked around the crowd and noticed a few Mod types amongst the Welsh but they were not very sharp looking and one of them had flares on. There were a few skins lurking amongst them but they looked like a lot of left-overs from 1969. The game was none too exciting either and as it dragged to a close only a single goal from Wrexham had provided any spark. Being one down darkened the atmosphere even further, and Mickey and Terry were scanning the crowd manically for any trace of the frontline but even they were starting to look disappointed. Chris consoled himself that at least the boredom had dulled the burning unease in his stomach that had raged since they left Euston. The final whistle brought further welcome relief.

As they piled out of the ground into the street Chris began to feel more positive. At least they had turned out and tomorrow it would be business as usual with the Mod disco at the Barge Aground to look forward to. There were some isolated slanging matches with Wrexham fans on the way to the station and a few choruses of 'We are I.C., I.C.F.' to the tune of D.I.S.C.O., but nothing major and as they approached the station Chris felt a huge surge of relief. It soon faded though as the group pushed onwards further into town. Chris pushed his way forward until he caught up with Dave.

'What's going on? Where are we going?'

'The frontline have got a boozer up here somewhere,' said Dave. 'If they are too pussy to turn up for a scrap then we will take it to them.'

Chris was gripped with panic. This was it. They might have avoided confrontation under the watchful eye of the North Wales constabulary and the comforting back up of the regular Hammers fans but now they were on their own. Thirty-odd strong and storming straight into Apache territory head on. This was not going to end well.

One of the top boys shouted back at them to split up and they broke away into smaller groups of four or five on both sides of the road. Although they looked a little more inconspicuous Chris still thought that they looked like a load of Southerners doing the Soho strut through some skanky Welsh backstreets. The main town centre faded into the distance as they pressed further on into an area of grey streets and worn out council houses. Word filtered back that they were looking for a pub called the Smithfield, and be ready.

'This is it, Chris,' said Billy with a forced smile.

'Yeah,' said Gaff, 'Time for action as the great man said.'

Dave half-turned around and stared at all three of them.

'Don't you fucking let me down, all right?'

'Yes Captain Mainwaring,' chuckled Billy.

Dave did not even hear him and he just kept walking, staring into the distance and seeking out the opposition with a violent relish. As they walked past a skip that was planted at the side of the road, Gaff began to poke around it as best he could without getting his white Fred Perry dirty. He pulled out two-foot-long lengths of copper piping and threw one towards Chris.

'What's this for?' said Chris naively.

'What do you think, you dozy bastard?' laughed Gaff. 'Do you think these Taffs ain't going to be tooled up?'

'Where's mine?' shouted Billy.

'Find something yourself, you lazy cunt,' said Gaff.

'Just as well I brought this then,' said Billy with a smile as he pulled a foot-long length of thick rubber hose from his jacket.

'What the fuck is that?' said Gaff. 'Have you come kitted out for a bit of washing machine repair?'

'It's filled with lead shot,' said Billy as he whacked it with a thud onto his outstretched palm. 'My brother makes them on the side at the factory he works in.'

'Very nice,' mocked Gaff. 'Made to measure thuggery.'

Chris could not understand his friends' light-hearted banter. His stomach was heaving and he could feel cold sweat across his forehead and palms. Suddenly the boys up front stopped and motioned to everyone to gather together at the end of the street.

'What's happening?' said Chris.

'We've found the Frontline's pub,' said one of the ICF foot soldiers. 'It's just around the corner. Get fucking ready.'

Chris took a deep breath and squeezed the copper pipe until his knuckles went white. He noticed Dave was close to the front of the group, nostrils flaring and almost hopping from foot to foot with anticipation. A shout went out and they all charged forward.

The Smithfield was an unremarkable boozer and not the hooligan headquarters Chris had imagined. Three herberts stood outside, smoking and nursing pint glasses, when a wave of East End fury enveloped them. The Welsh trio crumbled under the onslaught of fists and kicks that descended upon them and there was a spurt of blood across the pavement as someone ran a Stanley knife across the cheek of one of the prone figures. Chris, Billy and Gaff could not even get near the punters on the ground but from their position at the back of the mob they got a quick preview of what was to come. Bursting out of the bar and lounge doors came a flood of angry Welshmen. They may not have been waiting for the ICF but they were soon ready and the Frontline yobbos and other locals were all desperate to take a boot at the 'Cockneys'.

The ICF boys swung into action, kicking, punching and head-butting anyone that came through the door but the huge numbers pushed them back and a few of them were beaten to the ground. The mob that emerged from the lounge doors swung into an unconscious pincer movement and Chris, Gaff, Billy and the other geezers at the back had to turn around and face them. A stocky youth with tightly permed hair made directly for Chris who struck out automatically, forgetting about the copper pipe in his grasp. The metal cracked with a sickening thud across the curly-haired thug's nose and he dropped to the ground like a sack of potatoes. A stifling fear gripped Chris but he continued to lash out with his weapon at the wild-eyed hooligans that surrounded him.

Most of the ICF at the front were tooled up and after some wild screams of pain and flashes of bloodshed, some of the Smithfield locals lost their lust for violence and backed off a little. Although they continued to shout obscenities and throw the odd kick they let the hardcore Frontline members take the majority of the punishment. Billy, Chris and Gaff were still under pressure though and almost on their knees, fighting back but hopelessly outnumbered. Dave suddenly broke away from the ICF group and dived towards his friend's attackers swinging his hammer wildly. The solid weapon whacked against a few jaws and sent the mob back a few steps but one Wrexham fan was so intent on stamping Gaff into the ground that he never noticed Dave's frenzied attack until a hammer blow cracked his skull. The youth fell to the ground close to Chris and his eyes rolled backwards as thick streams of blood poured over his face. Chris felt a wave of bile rising in his stomach and the cacophony around him seemed muffled. Everything seemed to move in slow motion and appear blurred with only Dave in focus. Dave was wild-eyed, yelling and swinging his hammer at anyone who came close and almost smiling as he did it.

A high-pitched sound echoed in the background and suddenly everything snapped back into place.

'Old Bill,' someone screamed and both firms parted like the Red Sea.

'Get a fucking move on,' yelled Dave and he pulled Chris to his feet as a couple of police cars screeched to a halt just down the street.

The West Ham mob gathered everyone together quickly and moved back towards the train station throwing a few taunts back at the Wrexham firm as they went. They knew that the local plod would probably relish throwing them into the cells for a bit of variety and none of them were particularly keen to spend the rest of the weekend in Taffland. There were a few lads limping and holding sore faces but most of them were still buzzing from the scrap, leaping and jumping along the road already re-living each punch and kick. Dave had thrust his bloodied hammer back into his waistband and was receiving some hearty slaps on the back from Mickey and Terry for his crazed contribution to the fight.

Chris could still picture the unconscious stare of the youth who had fell close to him after receiving Dave's hammer blow to the head. He stopped and as he clung to a small wall at the edge of someone's front garden he retched violently. Only Billy and Gaff stayed behind to offer him any comfort.

Chapter Three

Sunday 19th of August, 1979

Dave pushed a burnt banger around the pool of watery baked beans that had been splattered onto his plate. His mum was not much of a cook and for tonight's evening meal she had been thoughtful enough to leave a delicate sprinkling of her fag ash at the side of the cremated toast which rested on a square of kitchen roll at his side. It wasn't so much cordon bleu as cordoned fucking off. She was a diamond though and not bad at ironing either – the suit, shirt and Peckham Rye that Dave was wearing were sharp as a razor. As he sat at the kitchen table with a clean tea towel tucked into his collar to protect his gear from the ravages of his mother's cuisine, he wondered how the evening would unfold at the Mod disco in the Barge Aground. He had been toe to toe with a few geezers in Barking before but there were not many boroughs in London where he had not had trouble. He gulped down some pork gristle and mentally shrugged his shoulders. He didn't really care one way or the other and those solitary two weeks he spent attending the Boy Scouts had at least taught him something. Be prepared.

There was the familiar thump of heavy work boots on the staircase and Dave's mood darkened immediately. His father stomped into the kitchen and made for the drawer under the sink. On the way there, his elbow banged against the back of Dave's head. It was no accident. As he raked through the drawer he cursed in frustration.

'Where is that fucking hammer? The hinge on the bog door is loose again. Do you have it?'

'What would I want with a hammer?' said Dave. 'I work in a fucking fruit market.'

'Yes you do,' growled his dad, 'And don't forget who got you that fucking job. I had to pull a lot of strings just to get your lazy arse off the dole.'

His dad liked to think he got Dave a job through his 'connections' but they were just hopeless boozers that he knew down at the local. The reality was that Dave was pointed in that direction by the Job Centre and the application and the successful interview was all down to him.

The kitchen drawer was slammed shut and Dave's dad leant back against the sink with his arms crossed. He stared at Dave, looking for faults or any opportunity to berate him. Old man Hughes was a bully, a fat fucking bully who kissed his supervisor's arse at work and looked for anyone that he could vent his impotent rage on.

'What's this?' he said as he pointed at the tea towel around Dave's neck. 'You wearing a bib again?'

'I'm keeping my shirt clean,' mumbled Dave. 'I'm going out.'

'What? On a Sunday? You've hardly been here all weekend.'

Dave put his fork down but held onto his knife as he met his father's venomous gaze.

'Well there is no point in hanging around this shithole,' growled Dave.

His dad leapt forward and slapped the side of Dave's head.

'You cheeky little shit. Me and your mother have sweated blood to give you a roof over your head and put steam on the table.'

Dave sat still but his knuckles whitened as he gripped the handle of his knife tightly.

'Mum might have done,' he retorted. 'All you have done is piss your wages up the wall or in the bookies.'

Mr Hughes was furious as he glared at Dave, who matched his stare. Cheeky cunt, he thought, he deserved a slap. He had been trying to knock sense into that little bastard since he was a nipper yet here he was now, all grown up and defiant as ever. He had filled out as well, a right big lump. Maybe he would wait until his wife came back home from the shops and he would have a word with her. Maybe even a little slap to remind her of her failings. Bringing up a yobbo instead of a polite young man? What could he have done? He was always at work and a few pints each night and the odd trip to the bookies was his right. They were the only things that made his life bearable.

The stare-off continued until finally Dave slammed down his knife and fork and tore off his tea towel.

'I'm off out,' he said as he kicked back the kitchen chair and stood up.

'Yeah, that's right,' yelled his dad. 'Fuck off with your mates. A bunch of fucking hairdressers the lot of you.'

Dave stood at the door for a few seconds, staring at his dad then he left the room with a snort.

'Don't forget your moped,' his father shouted then he stood alone in the kitchen listening to the echo of the front door slamming shut.

Chris pulled his Vespa to a halt next to Billy and Gaff's scooters on the wide pavement outside the Barge Aground pub. It was a plain, box shaped boozer that lurked on Barking Broadway and already a gleaming row of Vespas and Lambrettas were stretching down the street. By the look of it, most people's lazy Sunday afternoons were spent polishing their scooters and waiting for the pubs to open and most of the ageing chariots looked in showroom condition. A few Mods were hanging around outside the pub nodding to fellow devotees as they passed and smoking like test-lab beagles. The muffled thud of some classic Motown seeped onto the street and the beat spiked a little every time someone opened the boozer's door.

Chris took off his helmet and packed his gloves inside it. He felt a familiar tingle of excitement. The Barge was where it had all began for him and his mates. Only six months before they had been a nondescript bunch of ex-punks, football fans and left-over skins. Fashion was simple then – Doc Martens, t-shirts, Levis and Harringtons and they listened to a lot of Punk and a smattering of Ska. What united them all was a real love of The Jam. Some nights they would just sit in someone's house playing In The City, This Is The Modern World and All Mod Cons over and over while devouring the sleeve notes and album artwork.

One of Dave's hooligan acquaintances had mentioned that the Barge Aground would be their type of place and they eventually made the pilgrimage to darkest Barking. They got a few shady looks when they first stomped into the pub like a boot-boy advance party but they were soon ignored and the rest of the evening was a revelation. The place heaved with geezers in smart suits and birds with immaculate 1960s clobber. There was a real feeling that something exciting was happening and this gathering was at the heart of it. The following week they were all back with decent haircuts and better dressed and since then nothing had been the same. Chris and Billy loved it because of the sharp fashion and great looking girls, Dave loved it because a few of the regular faces were ICF and Gaff loved it because he was able to offload as many pills as he could on a good night.

'You recovered from yesterday?' Billy said to Chris.

'Yeah, must have been that dodgy meat pie at the Taffs' ground,' giggled Gaff.

Chris was ashamed but also angry. He had continued to be sick all the way back from Wrexham. Despite all the victory songs and high jinks on the train home he kept getting flashbacks of the Wrexham fan on the ground next to him. The image of his lifeless eyes and the dark blood dripping over his face after Dave's hammer blow made the bile rise in his throat again. Was he brown bread? Dave did not seem too bothered and there had been no Welsh filth despatched to Canning Town as far as he knew. The fucking idiot was probably sat up in a Wrexham hospital room boasting to his mates about how he took on the Cockneys. Unless he was in a coma or brain damaged. The thought made Chris shiver.

'It's just not my idea of a great Saturday,' said Chris. 'Rolling around in a gutter with a bunch of yobs. My gear was fucking ruined. Even me desert boots. It's a mugs' game.'

'But you're all right now though?' said Billy.

'Yeah, yeah,' said Chris with resignation.

'I'm not,' Gaff chipped in. 'I think some cunt bit me on the knee.'

Billy laughed.

'I told you mate. Those mountain folk are fucking cannibals, my old man read it in the Sunday papers.'

'It's all bollocks,' said Chris. 'There was so much more that we could have been doing.'

'Dave seemed to enjoy it,' said Billy with a shrug.

'Hold up, here he comes now. Mr Angry,' smirked Gaff.

Dave brought his scooter to an abrupt halt near his mates.

'All right ladies,' he sneered as he pulled his Lambretta onto its kickstand.

'Evening Dave,' said Billy. 'Any Welsh teeth marks on your knuckles this morning?'

'They got what the deserved,' said Dave. 'They won't forget that in a hurry.'

'If they can remember anything,' mumbled Chris.

'You what?' said Dave with a glare. Chris remained silent and sullen.

Dave took off his helmet, gloves and parka and straightened out his suit.

'The ICF lot thought we did pretty well up there.'

'Thanks commander,' said Billy sarcastically. 'Now are we going to stand out here talking tactics or get in and see if there are any loose gussets around?'

'I'm up for the gussets,' laughed Gaff as he led the way into the pub. Dave was still glaring at Chris as they walked through the door.

Before they had even got to the bar, Dave shot off to have a word with a few of the geezers who had been at Wrexham that were Barge regulars.

'Do you think he wants a drink?' said Chris.

'Fuck him,' said Billy. 'Let his new mates get a beer in. Just get three Forsythes for us.'

The trio got their drinks and they stood silently for a bit listening to the music and soaking up the atmosphere. The place was packed and the DJ was playing some old Chris Farlowe belter while searching in his record box for the next classic. No one cared that it was Sunday and the working week loomed on the horizon. In this embryonic scene every night was fair game for action. Traditional Friday and Saturday nights out only were for the squares. The fuckin' 9-5ers. Those little black and blue pills kept the party going and Gaff did more than most to keep things running.

'Think I might have a bit of business here,' said Gaff before he had even downed half of his pint. 'Back in a minute.' He moved off to the back of the pub where a few punters greeted him like an old friend. An old friend that fancied staying up to daybreak at least. Billy and Chris smiled knowingly at each other.

'He's fucking unstoppable,' smirked Billy. 'He could sell sand to the Arabs and snow to 'kin' Eskimos.'

'He's a bit blatant though, inn'e? He shows out a lot. He'd better watch he don't get nicked.'

'That's his problem,' replied Billy. 'He forgets that it's drugs. He just sees supply and demand. He was the same at school wasn't he? Flogging sweets and crisps at break time.'

'He's got to remember that he's not selling fucking Mars Bars anymore,' said Chris.

Billy started to rattle on about what they had got up to in school and Chris grunted in approval but he was not really listening. His eyes wandered over to where the DJ was and his heart skipped as close by were Charlotte and her clingy mates Barbara and Jill.

'Are you listening to me?' said Billy. He followed Chris' eye line over to the girls and smiled. 'You'd better get over there mate before they get snapped up.'

'I'll just say hello,' stuttered Chris then took a deep swig of his lager. 'I'll be back in a minute.'

'Yeah right, you take your time mate. Just one thing, you'd better put your cock back in your trousers – it's popped out.'

Chris instinctively looked down at his fly before he registered that Billy was taking the piss. Billy roared with laughter as Chris made his move.

As he approached the girls, Chris could see that Charlotte was looking even better than she had at the Wellington. She had a tight black mini-dress with white trim and it showcased every smooth curve on her shapely body. Fishnet tights, white ankle socks and a gleaming pair of loafers finished off her outfit perfectly in a way that made Chris catch his breath with excitement. Before Chris could speak Barbara noticed him lurking in the shadows.

'Hello Chris, come to join us again,' she said in a slightly mocking tone. Barbara was a nice enough girl but stick thin and she appeared to have no chin.

'Hi, how are you doing,' said Chris then he dried up.

'Hello stranger,' said Charlotte with a purr that made Chris's privates tingle. Jill said nothing and merely grimaced as if she had just sucked a vinegar-soaked lemon.

'Did you just get here?' Chris asked as he struggled to get the conversation rolling.

'Not long,' said Charlotte. 'What happened to your face?'

'Oh, it's nothing,' he said sheepishly. 'Some Welshmen got a bit rowdy at the football, that's all.'

'Oh yeah?' said Jill icily and gave him a look that would curdle milk.

The conversation between the four of them trundled on for a bit and then, either by accident or design, Jill and Barbara went to the khazi leaving Chris and Charlotte alone at last. Charlotte seemed to move a little closer and Chris felt a warm shiver down his spine

'That was you and your mates rolling around outside the Wellington on Friday, wasn't it?' she said.

'Yeah, it was,' Chris said quietly. 'Some local skins started it.'

'That's a mug's game Chris.' Charlotte touched the scratch on his cheek gently and smiled. 'All that bruising is no good for the complexion.'

Chris' stomach flipped with a bizarre mixture of terror and euphoria. It did not look as if she had written him off after all.

'A few of my mates got involved. I had to help them out.'

'That Dave Hughes is one of them, isn't he?' Charlotte asked. 'I've heard he is a fucking headcase.'

'He's all right,' Chris argued weakly.

'That's not what I've been told. I've heard he can start a fight in an empty room.'

'He's not that bad,' said Chris but he looked unconvincing.

Charlotte smirked and took a sip from her vodka and tonic. Her full glossy lips left a tantalising lipstick print on the glass.

'So what are you up to this week?' she asked. 'Fighting? Boxing? Beating up pensioners?'

Chris looked offended for a second before he realised that she was taking the piss.

'No. Nothing like that. Just getting ready for Southend.'

'Are you and your mates getting your coshes and knuckledusters polished?' Charlotte said with a laugh.

'Not really,' said Chris with a smile as he felt a surge of relief that they were having a decent conversation at last. 'I might put a new exhaust on my PX though.'

Charlotte swayed a little closer and her knee brushed lightly against Chris leg.

'What about Wednesday night? Do you think you can put your spanner down long enough to come to a Ska night with me?'

Chris's heart danced. He had been blindly searching for a way to ask Charlotte out and now it had landed on his lap.

'Yeah,' he blurted out then composed himself a little. 'Sure, aren't your mates going?'

'No. They are washing their hair that night.' Charlotte's lips curled into a wicked smile.

'Ok then,' Chris said, 'I can pick you up if you want.'

'No, that's all right. I'll meet you there. It's at the Ace Club in Brixton. About eight?'

'Sure, no problem. I'll be there.'

Charlotte squeezed Chris's hand and started to move off.

'I'd better go and find my mates, I'll see you then.'

'Okay,' was all Chris could manage as she walked away and as he drunk in her full figure and shapely legs he felt a warm 'Readybrek' glow all over. In his head he was already slipping her the goldfish. It didn't take long for his bubble to burst though as Dave strolled over and slapped him on the back roughly.

'Are you pumping that or what?' he said as he leered at Charlotte.

'We are going out. Yeah,' said Chris moodily.

'Oh right. Going out? Not fucking,' Dave chuckled darkly.

Chris looked furious and it was noticeable.

'All right mate, take it easy,' Dave continued. 'Nothing wrong with a bit of romance. As long as it doesn't get in the way, right?'

'Yeah, sure,' said Chris. 'It's nothing serious, just a night out.'

'Good lad,' roared Dave. 'You get in there my son. Like a rat up a drainpipe.'

Chris did not like Dave's tone and it made him question his feelings. He usually did not mind giving his mates a blow by blow account of what happened any time he had been with a bird but if he was lucky enough to get to grips with Charlotte he would not be telling these dirty bastards anything.

'I was talking to a few of the lads from yesterday. I think we could be going places with West Ham.'

'Oh yeah?' said Chris, unimpressed. Either Dave did not notice his mate's lack of enthusiasm, or he chose to ignore it.

'Yes indeed mate. If we put on a good show this season we could be in there.'

'So that's what you want to do every other Saturday?' said Chris. 'Travel up and down the country knocking lumps out of a bunch of yokel halfwits. Maybe get a kicking yourself?'

'What else is there?' reasoned Dave as he drained his pint and set down his glass at the bar. 'You've got to be part of something.'

'We are part of something. We're Mods and this scene is growing all the time. There's loads to do and you want us to spend every weekend bloodying our knuckles?'

Dave cast off Chris's plea with a dismissive sneer.

'Don't get me wrong mate. I love being a Mod but this thing won't last. Look at Punk. Rucking at football has been going on for fucking donkey's years. It's the oldest profession just behind prostitution. If we want to be a part of something that is where it's at.'

Chris was not convinced but he said nothing.

Dave glowered at him but then realised he was being a bit harsh.

'Look mate, I know it's not really your thing but we need to stick together. It's fucking rough round our patch. If you are on your own, you're fucked but if we're part of the ICF people won't take the piss. I don't want to be like my old man. A fucking nobody that just shuffles through life. I want people to know who I am. It's a respect thing.'

'But you're a Mod, Dave,' reasoned Chris. 'Surely that's enough. There's something special going on here and for the first time we are in at the ground floor, not chasing it up like Punk. Like you said, the football will always be around but this is happening now. Look at all this,' he said as he swept his arm around the packed room in a grand gesture. 'On a Sunday night as well. Then there's the Bridge tomorrow, the Lyceum later this week then Southend.'

Dave shrugged and seemed to relent a little.

'You're not going to see birds like these on the terraces,' Chris continued.

'Yeah, I suppose you are right,' sighed Dave then he smiled a little. 'I might need to get a hold of one of them soon. I've not had a bunk-up in weeks, my balls need a right emptying.'

As Dave leered at some girls who were dancing Chris got a couple of beers in. Chris returned and passed a pint glass to Dave.

'See anything you like?'

'That one with the blue crimplene dress is pretty tasty,' said Dave after a long gulp at his Forsyte Saga. 'Remember Barry Fry from school? I reckon that's his little sister. I've heard she is a right dirty slapper.'

Chris giggled and felt he was at last getting through to Dave. They had been mates for a while but recently Dave had seemed constantly preoccupied and moody. It did not take long for him to drift back though.

'Don't forget we've got Oldham on Saturday,' said Dave, still ogling the girl in the blue dress. 'Dirty cunts are coming down to us as well.'

Chris gasped in exasperation but Dave paid little attention.

'You can't fucking wait can you?' he said.

'No I can't,' said Dave loudly, then he noticed Chris' shocked expression. 'Look mate. I just love it all right? I always have. I remember when my old man took me to Upton Park for the first time. I think I was only about eight and I saw these fucking West Ham suedeheads tear right across the terracing and lay into a bunch of opposition fans. I can't even remember who they were but they took a right beating. It was a real buzz and I always remember my old boy laughing like fuck and shouting at the West Ham lads to stick the boot in harder. It was a real buzz but standing there with him I still felt safe. He was a good laugh back then, he wasn't always a cunt.'

'How is he these days?' said Chris.

'Still a cunt. Always either pissed or snoring on the couch. I don't know how my mum puts up with it. She should just go. All that till death do us part bollocks is old hat now. She should just leave him to stew in his own shit.'

'Then what would you do?'

'I'll be all right,' said Dave. 'I could get a flat or something. Anything to get away from him.'

Chris pondered for a moment as he struggled to say something supportive but it was too late. Mickey Thompson and Terry Harkins from the Glory Boys walked in and Dave was off towards them in a shot like a fucking groupie.

'I'll catch you in a bit Chris,' he said as he moved away eagerly. 'Just got to see about a bit of business.'

Chris sighed and leant against the bar. Dave was a good mate and someone that had always helped him out. Over the years they had had some fucking great laughs but now it seemed they were moving in different directions and he had a growing feeling of unease that things were changing at a rapid rate.

Chapter Four

Chris sat perched on the toilet seat, puffing on an ultra-thin roll-up with a copy of *Sounds* draped across his knees. His first day back at work after the weekend was usually shit but it was getting worse. The weekend itself had been a washout and his body still ached from the rumbles with the Morgans and those Wrexham Muppets. He had seen Charlotte twice though and it seemed that she had not quite given up on him yet, despite the bruises. The meet she had arranged with him for Wednesday night sort of sounded like a date but he was not entirely sure. His daydream came to an abrupt halt as his moody boss, Mr Norton, banged on the bog door.

'C'mon laddie, let's get this afternoon post section cleared. You're like a fart in a trance today. I was in the war alongside blokes with dysentery and they spend less time on the lavvy than you.'

The red-faced Scotsman was sweating profusely as usual and his beady eyes glared at Chris as he walked back into the post room.

'Come on son, you are as slow as shite on Mondays,' said Norton. 'What the hell do you get up to a weekends.'

Chris said nothing and started to load his mail trolley.

'In fact I've been meaning to speak to you,' Norton continued as he looked around the room. 'Now is as good a time as any. Come into my office.'

Although Chris' boss believed himself to be emperor of the post room his superiors obviously did not and his 'office' was no more than a desk and a few chairs in the corner of the basement surrounded by filing cabinets.

'Take a seat son,' said Norton, then snorted in disgust when he noticed that Chris had already helped himself to a chair. 'I've noticed a certain lacklustre performance on most mornings. You are like an old banger on a cold day. It seems to take you a bit of time to get going and we here at Shell Petrochemicals just can't have that.'

Chris struggled to contain a sneer. Norton talked as if he was the CEO of the company and not just another hired hand like the rest of them.

'This is a job that demands high performance,' droned the Scotsman. 'We are the lifeblood of this company. We keep this building connected to the world.'

He was rambling and Chris had heard it all before. Most of what he was spouting was from an old promotional film that the career teacher had shown in the gym hall to Chris and his classmates when they were in their final year at school.

'You see I need you in here fresh each morning, firing on all cylinders. Sometimes when you get here it is as if you have been out every night of the week.'

'I am out every night of the week,' Chris said bluntly.

'You see, that's no good son. The weekend is the time for play. During the week you should be staying in, saving your energy for the next working day ahead.'

Chris looked at Norton blankly. Staying in was not on the agenda. He had to be out there, he had to be seen. If he missed even a couple of Mod nights out he would be nothing, left behind, out of touch with what was happening and who the latest bands were. Things were moving so fast that if he even had a week off he was sure he would be a pariah.

Norton accepted that he was not going to get an answer but he carried on anyway.

'Don't throw your career away for a few nights out on the piss. If you stick in, who knows, you could have my job in twenty years.'

The thought of both still being there and being in Norton's job made Chris feel ill. His boss must have noticed the pained look on Chris's face because he sighed and gave him a dismissive wave.

'Off ye go laddie. Take that as your first verbal warning and get back to work.'

Chris got up and left, not bothering to push his chair back close to the desk.

'And buck your ideas up,' yelled the Scot after him but already Chris was around the corner, heading for the loading bay with his middle finger held aloft.

As the long day drew painfully to a close, Chris grabbed his parka and crash helmet from a coat peg in the mail room and headed down to the car park. He needed a quick respite to salvage something from the day so he thought he would nip into the Wellington on the way home just in case any of his mates were about. He had barely kicked into fourth gear by the time he arrived there and he was pleased to see Billy and Dave's scooters parked up in the usual spot. As he pulled his scooter onto its stand next to them he noticed that there was still some broken glass in the gutter where the Morgan boys had booted off his wing mirror. It was all quite now though and in the daylight it seemed odd that the street had been an arena for a brawl only three nights ago. There had probably been even more action since then as the Wellington attracted a colourful clientele and louts like the Morgan boys were always about looking for bovver. Chris shook his head slightly in dismay. It was all a load of bollocks.

Inside the boozer he found Dave and Billy at a table close to the bar door along with a scattering of hopeless boozers hunched over the bar and a few other tables filled with pre-dinner drinkers.

'All right boy?' said Dave. 'Come to join us before we head down to the Bridge House?'

'Yeah, mate,' said Chris. 'Just a quick one though then I'm going home to get dressed.'

'Fuck that,' said Billy. 'You look all right. Get a few down your neck and then we will go straight there. The Small Hours are playing tonight.'

'I've got my scooter though,' said Chris.

Billy and Dave looked at each other knowingly.

'And?' said Dave. 'Get the beers in, you poof. Let's get the night started.'

Chris went to the bar and eventually returned with three lagers.

'Hold up Dave,' said Billy. 'I know why he wants to get home and sorted out. He wants to look his best for that skinhead bird.'

Dave sniggered and took a deep slug from his glass.

'No it's not,' protested Chris. 'I don't even know if she will be there. I just want to get changed.'

'Bollocks. You take it too seriously,' said Billy as he leant back in his chair as if he was about to read out the gospel. 'You tell them what you want, take it and move on.'

'Nice,' said Chris sarcastically. 'That sounds like Jack the Ripper's diary.'

'Look, I quite fancied that little bird from Leytonstone with the blonde bob. You know her, sweaty Paul's sister? I asked her to come with me round the back of the Bridge a few weeks back and give me a gobble. I was up front, I think she appreciated my honesty. Either way it was job done and I've never spoke to her since.'

'Lovely. Honesty and a chin soaked in Harry Monk. Classy bird, and she must have really appreciated the experience,' sneered Chris.

'Whether she appreciated it or not, I got to spunk my load and move on. Everyone's a winner. Dave knows what I'm talking about. Right Dave?'

Dave said nothing as he was staring at a table of six geezers over at the other end of the bar.

'Dave,' Chris said loudly. 'What the fuck are you looking at?'

'Wake up mate, are you in a fucking trance or what?' said Billy.

Dave finally spoke but continued to stare at the guys who now knew they were being clocked.

'Those cunts over there, I'm sure they are Millwall.'

Chris let out a gasp of exasperation and thumped his pint down on the table.

'For fuck's sake Dave, leave it out will you. I'm still as sore as a weeping boil from the weekend and it would be nice to turn up at the Bridge House without being covered in claret for a change. I've fucked up two pair of strides already since we were last in here.'

Dave blanked him.

'Those cheeky bastards. Look at them. A bunch of fucking two-bob tickets and drinking in our pub.'

'It's only our pub when there's a band on. Most of the time it belongs to these old geezers,' said Chris as he waved towards the barflies and decrepit human shells that haunted the bar like lonely ghosts. They continued to sup in silence for a bit but Dave was still staring across the room and the geezers knew it. A few of them frowned a bit but they continued to talk amongst themselves. They were a similar age to Dave, Billy and Chris but soul boy types, smartly dressed but not Mod. A rough looking bunch as well but after about fifteen minutes still nothing had happened so Chris wrote it off as a teatime stare out that was not going anywhere and went to the bog. As soon as his piss started raining down on the pineapple cubes in the cracked urinal he knew he was wrong. Two of the blokes from the table at the back entered the toilet and immediately started a loud conversation between them about how bent Mods were. Chris knew it was intended for him and he strained to get last drops of urine out his bladder sharpish. He quickly tucked away his John Thomas but stood at the piss pot as if he was still in mid flow.

'They are all fucking benders as far as I know,' said one of the louts.

'Yeah,' said his mate, gesturing towards Chris. 'Look at this one, he's probably in here waiting to bum one of his mates.'

Chris sighed deeply. He had not intended to be scrapping again so early in the week. In fact, if he never got in a fight again it would be too soon but he knew what was coming. Better to strike first and at least try and get out of the confined space of the bogs. He tensed his stomach and reached into the bottom of the bowl for a handful of piss-soaked disinfectant cubes.

'Wash your mouth out you dirty cunt,' he screamed as he spun round and rammed the cubes into the face of the yob nearest to him. The geezer yelled and fell back, reeling from a combination of the blow to his mouth and the taste of bleach and urine. His mate looked a bit stunned for a second and that was all that Chris needed to send his toe crashing between the bloke's legs. He let out a muffled groan and sank to his knees before Chris's knee made contact with his jaw quickly after. As he fell forward, Chris made a dash for the door but the geezer with the piss-soaked chin was now fucking furious and not far behind him. Just before Chris reached the outer door of the toilet that led to the bar he twisted round and booted the inner door as hard as he could. He heard the satisfying crack of wood on nose as the door slammed into the face of his pursuer. As he burst back into the bar he was not sure if leaving the bog had been a good idea after all.

The whole room was in turmoil. He saw Dave and Billy screaming abuse from behind an upturned table as a hail of beer glasses and chairs rained down on them from the four remaining Millwall yobs. The barman and a couple of thickset navvy regulars were in the middle trying to calm things down while the barflies had retreated to an area of relative safety behind the fag machine. Chris stood like a rabbit in the headlights not sure of what direction to take, then the barman shouted at him as he moved towards the Millwall mob to stem the disturbance.

'Get your mates and get the fuck out... now!' he yelled.

'We ain't going anywhere,' shouted Dave. 'This is our pub.'

'I'm trying to save your arse you little cunt,' the barman yelled as he and the navvies pushed the Millwall lads back into a corner. 'Now get the fuck out.'

Billy got the message and made for the door with Chris but Dave stood defiantly, puffing out his chest and staring at the biggest Millwall lad.

'Come on Dave,' said Chris tugging at his mate's arm. 'For fuck's sake, let's go.'

The three of them left the pub and walked round to their scooters fairly quickly. Chris and Billy got on theirs and started to pull on their helmets but Dave was reaching into his tool box for a hammer. He gripped it firmly and stood in the street shaking with rage as the muffled chants of the Millwall boys seeped out of the pub.

'Listen to those cunts,' he seethed. 'I'm going back in.'

'Leave it Dave,' said Billy. 'We'll see them again.'

Chris was furious both at the stink of urine that was creeping up his arm and his mate's refusal to give up on a lost cause.

'Fucking hell Dave, just leave it. Do you want us barred from the Wellington as well as all the other boozers where you have kicked off? There will be nowhere else for us to fucking go soon.'

Dave paused for a few seconds then he turned and threw his hammer back into his scooter's tool box.

'All right,' he said as he slammed the tool box door shut and tugged on his helmet, 'But this ain't over.'

'It never fucking is with you,' said Chris quietly as he kicked his scooter into action and pulled sharply away from the kerb.

Chris did not look back as he pushed his PX into the rush hour traffic and headed straight for home. In his room he pulled off his suit and shirt and sniffed the sleeve on both of them with disgust. Both of them were stinking of piss, how was he going to explain that one to his mother? He decided to stash the dirty gear under his bed and worry about it later. Within minutes he had some fresh new gear on and he was heading for the front door. His mother spotted him in the hall as she peered from the kitchen.

'Where are you going? You've just got in,' she protested.

'I'm going to a gig at the Bridge House. I'll catch you later,' he yelled as he pulled on his parka.

'What about your dinner?'

'I'll get something later. See ya.'

Chris' mum was about to reply but the slam of the front door silenced her.

When Chris got to the Bridge House it was already packed and Dave and Billy had obviously gone straight there as they were already holding court alongside Gaff and a bunch of other local Mods, filling them in on what had gone on at the Wellington. No doubt Dave was attempting to stir up a posse for a return engagement with the Millwall firm. Chris caught their eye with a wave then gestured that he was going to the bar for a drink. As he stood amongst the crowds waiting to be served, he took a good look around the venue. It was heaving with punters and there must have been around four hundred Mods and assorted hangers-on crammed into the venue. Since the Mods' Mayday gig, this place had become ground zero for the scene and it was growing every week. Mod night was an essential part of the week. All the faces, all the wannabe faces and all the bands now made their way to Canning Town every Monday. To his manor and to this boozer, a pub that many believed was still a haunt only populated by brawling dockers. That lot were all a distant memory, this was a place for his generation now. There were even a few curious looking punters who had just came along to see what all the fuss was about. Chris beamed with pride. Less than a year ago Monday nights would have consisted of a night in front of the box with his mum and dad watching Kick Start but now he had all this, right on his doorstep. It was not much of a looker, in fact the rumour was it was about to be condemned so the owners were not investing too heavily on its maintenance, but the atmosphere was electric and on Monday nights it was all theirs.

'All right Chris,' said Dave, slapping his mate on the back. 'You been home to get changed? That Millwall lot barely touched you.'

'They jumped me in the bogs,' Chris moaned. 'There was piss all over my suit.'

Dave stifled a laugh as he noticed Chris was not in the mood.

'Fucking liberty takers. I've been speaking to a few of the lads. We're going to sort them scabs out.'

'Not tonight mate,' said Chris with a groan. 'Why have we got to be scrapping every day?'

'All right Ghandi, keep your nappy on. There's plenty time. It can wait for another day. Just watch the band and fucking cheer up.' Dave scowled and made his way back to Gaff, Billy and the other Bridge regulars.

Chris stayed at the bar and as The Small Hours came onstage he felt a small buzz but nothing like the usual thrill he usually felt when seeing a new Mod band play. This was usually his greatest night of the week but Dave had already taken a right shine off it... again. His mood began to mellow though as The Small Hours rattled through their classy set. They were a rowdy five piece and they seemed to have brought a lot of new punters with them. That's how things went at the Bridge. Another week, another great new band and even more faces. Before long, Chris was down near the front of the stage jumping around wildly. As the night progressed Billy and Gaff, and eventually Dave, joined him as they bounced around in the dark. After the gig was over and they had all gone their separate ways, Chris made it home and crashed out on his bed fully clothed The final black bombers rush had washed away all the shit from the past few days and he slipped into a deep, satisfying sleep.

Chapter Five

The cheap digital alarm clock echoed around Chris' bedroom but he was already awake and staring at the ceiling. He silenced its tinny bark with a slap of his hand. Monday had been a shit day, a bad shift at work followed swiftly by a kick in the nuts from that Millwall mob. Only the lively performance from The Small Hours at the Bridge House had stopped the beginning of the week from being a total disaster. His body ached and every last trace of black bombers had left his system leaving him lethargic. The thought of getting out of bed filled him with dread, so when his mum began to yell upstairs informing him there was someone on the phone for him he was furious.

He dragged himself into the hall and shouted at his mother.

'Who is it?'

'I don't know genius. Speak to them and you'll find out,' she trilled from the kitchen. 'Although I think it might be Gary.'

Chris picked up the phone and peered fuzzily at himself in the hall mirror.

'Chris?' came Gaff's voice. 'Sort your mother out mate. No one calls me Gary anymore.'

'That's your name ain't it,' said Chris.

'Only to the nearest and dearest mate. Gaff's my street name.'

'Street name? Fuck off, what do you want?'

'You're not at work yet I take it?'

'I wouldn't be fucking speaking to you now if I was,' said Chris angrily.

'Christopher! Mind your language at home,' yelped his mother in the background.

'Yes Christopher,' giggled Gaff. 'No rude words at home, you cheeky cunt.'

Chris began to feel a burning desire to get back to bed.

'What do you want Gaff?'

'I don't want anything mate, I want to give. To give you an opportunity to earn sixty knicker today. Easy money and we will be done by early afternoon.'

'What is it this time?' groaned Chris.

'A prime retail opportunity. A chance to offer the good housewives of London some of the finest housewares on the market.'

'You're going on the knock again,' said Chris bluntly.

'If you want to call it that mate. I think of it more as an opportunity to serve the community... and make a little bit of moolah while we are at.'

Chris pondered for so long that Gaff thought the line had gone dead.

'Are you still there mate?'

'Yeah,' said Chris. 'All right. Are Billy and Dave coming?'

'Of course brother. They are busy writing sick notes as we speak.'

Chris was sick of his work so a bit of cash in hand and a day away from that porridge-munching Jock bastard Norton seemed like a good solution.

'When can you pick me up?'

'Half-nine mate. And make sure you look presentable. See you then,' said Gaff and hung up.

Chris placed the phone back down gently then yawned and stretched. A quick shave, a shit and a shoe shine and he would be ready.

'Mum,' he shouted into the kitchen. 'Could you phone my work? I don't feel all that well.'

Chris was ready and waiting at the end of his street, puffing on a fag and already wondering if he had made the right decision. He knew that going 'on the knock' was a common money spinner around many parts of the country. Faceless gang masters would organise vanloads of herberts to descend on neighbourhoods and provide them with cut-price tat to sell door-to-door at vastly inflated prices. The 'salesmen' would be encouraged to peddle some sob story about their personal disabilities or claim they were raising money for some charity. Being an ex-offender trying to pay back their debt to society with parole office supervision was another standard. At the end of the day it was just a money-spinner designed to stay at least close to lawful practice. As the 'knocker' walked backed up the garden path with the householder's cash jammed in his pocket, the lucky consumer would be left with a handful of shit quality tea towels and dishcloths that would evaporate after their first use. It certainly was not an honest day's work but it was lucrative, and residents could be persuaded to part with their hard-earned through a combination of charm and mild threat or simply because they wanted some horrible oik off their doorstep.

As a large white mini-bus pulled to a halt in Chris' street with a screech, he threw down his dog-end and got in. He squeezed his way to the back and sat down with Gaff, Billy and Dave. There were about ten other geezers in the van including a few desperadoes Chris had been to school with, some pikey types, Mickey Thompson, a few of his Glory Boy mates that they had been shadowing all weekend, and a couple of guys whose accents were so thick Chris was not sure whether they were Irish or Krauts.

'Where are we off to?' Chris asked Gaff.

'It's a treat for you today Chris,' smiled Gaff. 'A nice trip south of the river to sunny Chislehurst; Kent's premier spot for horny public schoolgirls and sexually frustrated housewives.'

'Yes indeed,' said Billy while rubbing his thighs lasciviously. 'They will be frothing themselves up now, ready for some young cock. It will be like Confessions of a Window Cleaner all over again.'

'You've been watching too many films you dirty bastard,' said Chris. 'More likely they will set the dogs on us.' Chris looked towards Dave for a response but his friend just stared out the window moodily. 'Are you all right mate?'

'He's still pissed off that we got our arse kicked by Millwall last night,' Billy chipped in.

'That was a fucking liberty,' spat Dave. 'We should have got a few geezers and gone back there. There were loads at the Bridge who were up for it.'

'Yeah, they said they were up for it but after the band finished they soon melted away,' said Chris.

'Fucking liberty,' Dave mumbled. For the rest of the guys it was no more than just another slanging match in a boozer but for Dave it was always much more. He was determined to avenge every slight, every insult, every hand that had been laid on him in anger. He could not let it go and his mates knew that it was better to let him simmer than attempt to persuade him otherwise.

It did not take long to get across the river and soon the council housing and industrial estates gave way to the wide tree-lined avenues and neatly trimmed gardens of North West Kent. As they passed a local college someone pointed out the name, Beaverwood School For Girls, and they all had a giggle. One of the pikeys could not help but state the bleedin' obvious.

'I'd give their beavers some wood,' he guffawed but it did not raise a titter.

'Yeah, good one mate,' said Gaff sarcastically. 'If I wasn't doing this I would be giving your old mum some wood.'

'Cheeky fucking yid,' spat the geezer as he tried to reach across the van and get a grip on Gaff. Dave was onto him in a flash and pushed him back into his seat roughly.

'Shut your fucking mouth and sit down.'

The bloke was a big lump and looked as if he was ready for a scrap but he changed his mind when he saw Dave's staring, red-rimmed eyes and settled back into his seat sullenly.

'Yeah, take it easy you mug,' one of the Glory Boys shouted at Dave's adversary. 'We're not going to make much fucking money if you turn up at the front door covered in blood.'

The van parked up a little bit away from the streets that they intended to target and the geezer next to the driver pointed to some boxes near the back.

'Right, everyone take a bag each from in there. There's fucking loads of gear in them and a slip with guide prices. We want 30 sovs a bag for them when you're done so whatever you make above that goes in your pocket. If you manage to flog the whole bag come back here and we'll give you another one.'

'I hope it's good gear this time,' said one of Chris' old school mates. 'That last lot was well snide.'

'Don't you fucking worry about the quality,' said the driver's mate. 'Just get it flogged. By the time they find out it is shit we will be well gone and we probably won't come back here for another six months or so.'

The lads all grabbed their bags and piled out of the van.

'Right split up,' said Mickey Thompson. 'We don't all want to be treading on each other's toes. Small groups and a street each. You coming with us Dave?'

Dave almost leapt at the opportunity then he held back.

'I'll go down here with my mates,' he said sheepishly. 'I'll catch you back at the van.'

'Fair enough,' said Mickey and then he and the rest of the Glory Boys moved off down the street.

'Catch you back at the van,' mocked Gaff once they were out of earshot.

'Shut the fuck up,' said Dave slapping Gaff roughly on the back with his bag of household tat. 'Let's start down here.'

'Whoa, whoa,' said Gaff as they started to move down the street. 'After me surely. Watch the master in action and learn.'

'Gaff,' said Chris holding his bag of cheap goods up, 'If you can sell this shit you deserve a knighthood.'

Despite the poor quality of the goods most of the tat seemed to sell itself and within the first hour Chris had cleared most of his bag and his pockets were jangling with spare change. Gaff caught him coming out of a garden after yet another sale and he looked a bit pissed off.

'Are you sure you are selling that and not just dumping it in the bushes?' he said with a hint of jealously.

'Yeah,' said Chris, 'They seem to be well up for it.'

Gaff snorted and made off quickly for the next house, refusing to be outdone on the sales front. The truth was that most of the old ladies and housewives seemed to be fairly glad to have a tidily dressed young man visit them, and Chris had been able to shift most of his gear without too much of a hard sell. Despite all the sniggering in the van, most of the householders seemed lonely rather than horny although a couple of snooty bints had slammed the door in his face. As he handed over the shoddy goods he did feel an occasional twinge of guilt but that did not stop him from jamming the cash in his pocket then moving on to the next door.

As he left one of the gardens and walked past the house where Gaff was laying the spiel on a woman who looked like Olive from On The Buses, he found Dave leaning against a small wall and staring across the street.

'All right Dave?' said Chris. 'Are you taking a breather?'

Dave was peering at two young lads on the other side of the road who were browbeating a householder into buying some shady cleaning materials. One of the lads was short and stocky while the other one was a tall streak of piss.

'They weren't in our van were they?'

'I don't think so,' said Chris. 'I think I would have remembered Little & Large.'

'What the fuck are they doing here then?' growled Dave. 'This is our patch.'

'I wouldn't say that,' said Chris. 'We've hardly got a hawker's license for the whole of Chislehurst.'

'Well we are here now,' said Dave. The two lads had finished prying some money from the home owner and they were back on the main road before they noticed Dave and Chris. Billy and Gaff had just finished clinching their deals and they were close by.

'Oi,' Dave shouted over to them. 'We are working this street. Piss off.'

'Fuck you,' shouted the smallest geezer. 'We got dropped here, this is our run.'

'You are not with our lot,' said Chris. 'Where are you from?'

'New Cross, why what's it to, you poofter?' said the dwarf puffing his chest out and bringing himself up to his full five foot three.

'Are you fucking Millwall?' said Dave as he dropped his bag of goods on the street and started to clench his fists.

'Why? Who wants to know?' said the taller guy but it looked as if he realised Dave already knew the answer.

Dave was across the road in seconds, not running but striding at a fast pace. He slapped the tallest guy across the ear and grabbed his bag of stock from him.

'Get the fuck out of here you dirty scabs, we are working this estate,' he spat. Chris, Gaff and Billy followed him over quickly and got to Dave's side just as he was kicking the little geezer up the arse. Both of the Millwall lads walked away quickly but the small guy could not resist a parting shot.

'You wait there, you cunts,' he piped up. 'We'll be back.'

'We're not going anywhere,' shouted Dave. 'Now piss off.'

When the lads were gone Chris, Dave, Billy and Gaff stood together.

'What do you think?' said Chris. 'There must be more of them. They are not going to send just two geezers out on the knock.'

'Maybe we should see the others,' said Billy. 'There must be some back at the van by now.'

'We don't need anyone else,' said Dave. 'We will deal with them if they come.'

'It wouldn't hurt to give Mickey Thompson and his mates a shout. Would it?' said Gaff as he played Dave like a flute.

Dave didn't even know he was being manipulated but the idea of another tear-up with the Glory Boys beside him was appealing.

'Let's go back to the van then, but watch your back.'

Mickey and his mates were indeed back at the van, puffing fags and comparing what they had sold. The rest of the group also turned up alongside Chris, Dave, Billy and Gaff. The two guys in the van looked pleased to see a few empty stock bags already and they were collecting their share of the cash.

Dave could not wait to break the good news.

'There's a fucking mob of Millwall back there on the knock as well.'

'You what?' said Mickey and turned to the van driver and his mate. 'Do you know about this?'

'Must be some other group,' said the driver. 'Everyone knows this is our patch. Fucking liberty.'

Mickey turned back to Dave and flicked his fag-end into the gutter.

'I hope you dealt with it.'

Dave held the lanky Millwall geezer's bag out in front of him.

'Too right. I taxed him for this, kicked him in the arse and told them both to fuck off.'

'I think they want it back,' said Gaff with a dry giggle and pointed up the street.

About a dozen Millwall knockers were lined up across the road like something out of High Noon and Chris knew instantly that this argument was not going to be settled with reasoned discussion. It was time to get his knuckles red again and funnily enough after all the trouble of the past week he was actually ready for it. Why not? He had been kicked about from Waterloo to Wrexham and back and he was still standing. Another tear-up would not make any difference and it was more exciting than pushing that post trolley around for another day.

'Come on then you cunts,' he shouted, and Billy, Gaff and even Dave looked a little shocked but it was all it took to send both firms crashing into each other. The curtains began to twitch furiously as the householders peeked out on to their cosy, tree-lined street to investigate the racket only to see two dozen lads knocking lumps out of each other just beyond the rose bushes and neatly clipped lawns. The telephone exchange at Chislehurst police station must have been lit up like a fucking Christmas tree.

Soon there were blood-stained tea towels and dishcloths strewn across the road with what looked like a few teeth as well. The Millwall lot obviously had not planned a full toe-to-toe with a rival firm on a sunny Tuesday afternoon and they seemed slightly taken aback. Dave and the Glory Boys were right in amongst them kicking, punching and head butting anything that got in their way. Bags of household wares were being swung around as weapons and bodies were being slammed into parked cars, lampposts and garden walls. The pikeys from the Canning Town van were either confused or had another agenda and they both tore into Gaff. Dave and Billy fought them off but the toe-rags were obviously friends of the driver as they retreated to the van and drove off.

Chris knew that they were now sitting targets for both the police and any of the remaining Millwall louts in the area and he enlisted Billy and Gaff's help to spread the word. Luckily most of the Millwall lot were now decked out so Dave, the Glory Boys and the rest of their sales team were persuaded to step back after they had dished out a few final kicks to the bodies on the ground. After a few West Ham chants, they left the street and started walking away from the action. They could not have looked more out of the place if they had tried – nine battered & bruised geezers stomping down the street buzzing with adrenalin.

'Where's the van?' shouted Dave.

'They fucked off,' said Billy. 'Them two pikeys had a go at Gaff then done one.'

'We're bound to get nicked,' said one of the other lads from the van. 'There's nowhere to hide here.'

'We ain't going to hide,' said Mickey. 'We'll walk straight through to the station and get out of town.'

'Where is the station?' said Billy.

'I don't fucking know,' said Mickey angrily. 'Just keep walking.'

Billy looked furious but he said nothing.

'That fucker with the van is getting it when I get back,' seethed Dave as they turned the corner into yet another identically neat suburban street. 'Who was he?'

'I don't know,' said Gaff. 'Just a geezer I met in a pub.'

'He has fucking dropped us right in it,' said Billy.

One of the Glory Boys brought the group to a sudden halt.

'Whoa, hold up, look over there.'

At the end of the street were two battered transit vans crawling along the road. Their side doors were open and about a dozen geezers lurked inside each one. Even from a distance it was clear to see they were seriously tooled up with baseball bats, pick-axe handles and crowbars.

'In here,' barked Mickey huskily and the group ducked behind a privet hedge into someone's garden.

'What the fuck are we going to do?' said one of the old schoolmates. 'Do we make a run for it?'

'Fuck that,' said an older Mod. 'I'm not having it off on my toes from those cunts. Besides they've got vans. Unless you can run like Seb Coe you're fucked.'

Mickey surveyed the area like a general then he noticed an arched passage between the house behind them and its identical neighbour.

'We'll nip through the back gardens and come around behind them,' he ordered . 'If you see anything that even resembles a tool on the way fucking grab it.'

They crashed through the passage and worked their way steadily through every garden. Anyone peering out of their window would have seen a group of louts trampling their flower beds and pinching anything that could be utilised as a weapon on the way. Luckily, most of houses seemed to be commuter homes and the lad's presence only garnered a few dog barks. They climbed fence after fence before finally gathering behind a high garden gate close to the road where the vans had been. Mickey gestured for them to shut up then he peeked quickly over the fence and ducked down again.

'They are still there,' he said quietly. 'Is everybody tooled up?'

Most of them nodded. Chris smirked nervously. All he could find was the metal pole from a swingball set and the fucking ball was still attached. He gave the heavy nylon cord a tug but it was on tight.

'Have you got your blade Terry?' Mickey asked his mate who nodded as he pulled out what looked like a World War II commando dagger. 'Do you reckon you could get to the van at the front and do the tyres?'

'I'll try my best,' said Terry then he opened the gate slightly, peered out then ran to the other side of the road.

Mickey shut the gate quietly and held his finger to his lips to silence the rest of them. Chris was getting alarmed. This was getting out of hand. A tear up in the street was one thing but these geezers were planning it like a military ambush.

'Oi you little cunt,' came a shout from across the street. 'Get the fuck away from our van.'

'Let's fucking do it,' yelled Mickey as he flung open the gate and ran into the street with a broken pick-axe handle in his grip. They all piled out of the garden and ran towards the two van loads full of Millwall. The van at the front was listing heavily to the right as both tyres on the driver's side were flat as pancakes. Terry had obviously done his job well as four geezers were trying to take a swipe at him but he stood with his back to a wall swinging his blade wildly. Some of the Millwall lads had put their weapons down and they were inspecting the shredded tyres when the mob descended on them. Once again the clatter of bodies and violent shouting must have left the Chislehurst locals wondering whether their leafy suburb had recently become a war zone. Mickey and his mates set about the blokes who were trying to get to Terry while everyone else took a swing at whoever was nearest. Most of the weapons in use were soon dropped or thrown at opponents and a massive Barney began.

During the melee, Chris noticed Mickey Thompson running towards the van at the back which still had its tyres intact. Mickey let go a whoop of delight when he discovered that the keys were still in the ignition and he started the rusty beast first time.

'Get in,' he yelled and revved the engine wildly.

Most of the Canning Town mob did not need to be asked twice and they broke away from the tear-up and made for the side door of the van. Dave was still wrestling on the ground with the skinny geezer he had taxed earlier but Billy ran across the road and booted the beanpole off of his mate. Dave looked ready to continue but Billy dragged him towards the van which was already starting to move off. As soon as they got on board and slammed the sliding door shut Mickey whooped with delight and drove straight towards the Millwall mob. They dived out of the way but Mickey caught the back lights of the other van with the stolen van's bumper. The red and clear glass disintegrated then Mickey reversed the van quickly and took another ram straight into the other vehicles back door.

'For fuck's sake,' someone yelled. 'Let's get out of here.'

'All right, all right,' said Mickey almost casually as he reversed back once more then shot forward into the street leaving the furious Millwall lads behind in a cloud of diesel smoke.

Mickey Thomson pulled the hijacked van to a halt outside the flats on Fords Park Road.

'Is this your gaff Dave?' he asked.

'Yes mate, but drive on a bit would you, I'm not getting out here.'

'Fuck that,' said Mickey. 'It's not a fucking taxi service. We've got to get this thing dumped somewhere quick and put a match to it.'

Dave and Gaff were the last ones in the back and Mickey and Terry were upfront. The two of them got out and slammed the sliding side door shut.

'Take it easy lads,' said Harry. 'Better get some rest. We've got Oldham at home on Saturday. Northern cunts.'

Mickey gave a brief wave and the van sped off leaving Dave and Gaff standing next to some bin bags that had been left in the street. Dave took a kick at one of them and it burst open spilling rubbish onto the pavement.

'Fucking dump,' growled Dave.

'Well that don't help,' smirked Gaff. 'Keep Britain tidy you moody bastard.'

Dave almost smiled.

'What are you up to?' he asked.

'I'm off home mate,' said Gaff, 'And I've got to pick up a little something along the way.'

'You're not stilling buying pills from that fucking greaser are you?' moaned Dave.

'It's strictly business mate. And anyway, he's not that bad a bloke. What's the difference anyway? I listen to Mod music, he listens to Ted music.'

'There's a big fucking difference. Those cunts are going to be trying to wrap a bike chain round your head down at Southend on Bank Holiday Monday.'

'Nah,' said Gaff. 'It will probably end up like usual, a load of punters running and shouting at each other the old bill in the middle.'

Dave sneered as he started to light a fag.

'There will be action all right. Don't you worry about that, I'll make sure of it.'

Gaff was starting to tire of Dave's constant talk of violence. A bit of a dust-up was good fun now and again but Dave was dragging them into conflict almost on a daily basis and it was bad for business. Even the most devoted speed freak was wary of coughing up good money for a handful of blood-soaked bombers.

'Anyway, I'd better go,' said Gaff.

'Let's go for a livener mate, just the one,' said Dave.

Gaff was unsure.

'I don't know Dave, I've definitely got things to do.'

'Just the one mate, please.' Dave seemed almost desperate not to go home.

'Well okay,' Gaff said in a resigned tone. 'But could we stick with just the beer. I'm not in the mood for a bar-room brawl on the side.'

'Of course mate,' said Dave with a hint of a smile. 'I will try my best.'

Despite persuading Gaff to stay in the boozer for a few jars, Dave found himself heading back home around seven o'clock. Although it was a sunny evening, the streets around Dave's flat were fairly quiet. He stopped for a moment on the little concrete square outside his block and finished his fag. He raked through his pockets and fingered the collection of £5 and £1 notes that he had gathered from the good folks of Chislehurst. He had made about a pony, £25, but his fairly new Fred Perry V-neck was fucked after that fight with the Millwall knockers so he was not really that much better off. The thought that maybe all this scrapping was a bit of a waste of time flitted through his mind but he quickly chased it away. He felt his shoulders and chest tense up a little as he headed up the stairs to his flat.

He had barely put his key in the front door before he could sense the tension in the air. As he walked into the cramped hallway he could see his father in the front room staring at the TV, almost refusing to greet Dave's homecoming with any response. Dave walked into the kitchen where his mother was hovering over the cooker but not really doing anything.

'You all right mum?' he asked.

'Yes son,' she said quietly. 'Do you want a cup of rosy?'

'Yeah, all right.' Dave sat down at the small Formica table that was jammed between the fridge and the window. He watched his mother fill the kettle and even the effort of that seemed to cause her pain. As he looked around the kitchen he noticed a plate in the kitchen sink that was still loaded with food but smashed to pieces. His stomach tightened.

'You sure you are ok,' persisted Dave.

'Yes, son. I'm just feeling a bit rough. Not had my fags,' she said and attempted to laugh a little but even that looked as if it caused her discomfort.

Dave noticed right away that her cigarettes and lighter were where they usually were on the window ledge. The kettle clicked off and his mum reached up to the cupboard over the sink for some cups. The stretch made her gasp and as she steadied herself on the worktop she unwittingly lifted her top a little to clutch close to her ribs. Dave noticed immediately that her ribs were bruised and raw. The bastard. Page number one in the wife beaters' handbook – don't leave marks that the neighbours can see. He leapt from his chair and grabbed the biggest knife he could from the kitchen drawer. Before his mum could even yell he was in the front room.

His dad was obviously prepared because, as Dave burst into the room, he was out of his seat already and lurking near the door. Before Dave could even swing the blade his dad had knocked it from his hand with a heavy blow from something. It was a twelve-inch-high football trophy that Dave had won back in Primary school when he was the team captain. His Dad swung it again and the blow hit Dave across the forehead and he crashed to the floor. Dave's dad had been a bit of a lad in his younger days but he was old and flabby now and although he still liked a bit of the rough stuff he preferred it when his victims did not hit back. Dave was more than ready to hit back and even though his head burned with pain his hatred was stronger. With his back on the carpet he lashed out with his foot and his blood-stained hush puppy sunk deep into his father's groin. His old man fell to his knees and his eyes rolled back in pain but, before Dave could get to his feet, his dad managed to fall forward and grab his legs. Dave started to punch his dad again and again on the head but his old man was made of stern stuff and slowly dragged himself up Dave's torso until he was sitting on his chest and he managed to pin Dave's arms to the floor with his knees. He was also driven by hate. He had brought this little bastard into the world and he would take him out if he had to. Dave was writhing wildly on the floor but he was helpless under his father's weight and he could only spit out curses.

'You ungrateful little shit,' hissed his father as his hands gripped around Dave's throat. 'I've done everything for you and this is what I get? When I was your age, I would have laid out little poofs like you and your mates on the cobbles.' His eyes were wild and the veins on his forehead looked ready to burst. 'The best part of you ran down your mother's leg.'

'No John, no!' screamed Dave's mum as she ran into the room and swung a frying pan directly at the back of his dad's head. The stainless steel cracked against his skull and he fell forward pushing all the air from Dave's chest. Dave struggled to breathe as the dead weight bared down on him and his throat still ached from the choking grip that had been pressing against his windpipe. Dave's mum helped drag the unconscious body from on top of her son and, when he was free, Dave rolled onto his side and started to suck in lung-fulls of air.

'You have to go son,' said his mum. 'Please son, I'm sure the police will be on their way.'

'But what about you, mum?' gasped Dave.

'I'll be all right,' she sneered. 'This piece of crap has laid his hands on me for the last time.' She seemed to have put every ounce of resentment and fear that had built up over the years into that single blow. 'Please son,' she said as she flopped down into his dad's chair still clutching the frying pan, 'Pack some stuff and get out. Just until this is sorted.'

Dave struggled to his feet, still stroking his aching throat, and he looked over his dad's body.

'Is he dead?'

'He's too fucking stubborn to die son. He's still got misery to give someone.' She let out what sounded like a contented sigh. 'Well it won't be bleedin' me. I'll call the ambulance in a bit. Bring me my fags son.'

Dave went through to his room and packed some gear into a sports bag along with a bundle of cash that he had hidden under his mattress next to his collection of jazz mags. When he was done he went back into the front room to say goodbye to his mum. He kissed her on the forehead and told her he would be in touch.

'You take care, boy,' she said quietly. 'I'm sorry about all this. Just remember... I love you.'

Dave felt a rush of emotion but he forced it back down as he headed for the door. He looked around the room as he went. His mother was sitting smoking and looking completely spent. His father was till spark out on the floor, moaning slightly and with a dark crimson stain growing on the back of his head. In the background he could hear the distant wail of an ambulance. What a fucking state. Talk about Hammer House of Horror. He slammed the front door behind him and walked out into the golden evening light.

Billy lived a few streets away from Dave but his home was markedly different. Although his end-terraced council house was not much bigger than Dave's flat what it lacked in size it made up for in atmosphere. Billy was the youngest of four brothers and his home was almost a halfway house for any passing herberts that knew the boys. Mrs Keegan could always be found in the kitchen knocking up food for whoever happened to be there at the time. Billy's dad was a long-distance lorry driver but even in the rare periods he spent at home he was pretty accommodating, sitting on his chair next to the TV passing comments on whatever was showing and always willing to share his fags or booze with the constant stream of visitors.

While the rest of the family were roaring loudly in the front room at an episode of Mind Your Language, Billy had retired to his room after a bath and he was lying on his bed lightly touching the bruises and cuts he had acquired over the past few days. In between wincing and stretching his tired joints he flicked through a couple of copies of the Maximum Speed fanzine that he had picked up at the Bridge House. He had barely got comfortable before his mum began yelling up the staircase.

'Billy, come down here. It's Betty Hughes's son come to see you.'

Billy did not respond but he sighed and started to pull on a pair of strides that were hanging over the chair next to his bed.

'What's your name, son,' Billy's mum said to the visitor quietly before yelling once again. 'It's Dave.'

'Send him up then,' Billy shouted angrily.

'Up you go son,' said Mrs Keegan. 'I'll bring you a cup of tea.'

Dave walked into the bedroom just as Billy was pulling on a clean t-shirt.

'You going somewhere?' said Billy nodding at the bag Dave was carrying.

Dave said nothing and stood by the door clutching the bag.

'Well sit down then,' said Billy pointing at his brother's bed a few feet from his. 'Don't hang about like the fucking shadow of death. What's happening?'

'I've left home,' Dave said and flopped down on the bed. 'I think my Dad's in hospital.'

'You didn't hit him did you?' said Billy.

'I didn't get the chance. The old bastard was choking me and my mum hit him with a frying pan.'

'Fuck off,' said Billy with a smile. 'You've been watching too much Benny Hill. Either that or you are taking the piss.'

'It's true,' said Dave. 'I'm fucking done there. I'm not going back while that cunt is in the house.'

Billy lay back on the bed and fumbled for the packet of fags on his small bedside cabinet. He threw one to Dave and lit his own.

'So where are you going to go then?'

Dave took a deep draw from the cigarette and stared down at the floor.

'Oh, I see,' said Billy. 'Do you want to crash here?'

'Just for a couple of nights.'

Billy let out a long lungful of smoke in a smooth whoosh.

'Fair enough mate,' he said. 'It's fucking mental in here anyway. You'll fit right in. You'll have to sleep on the floor though, between the two beds.'

'Thanks mate,' said Dave. 'It means a lot.' Saying anything that even vaguely sounded like gratitude was a real strain for Dave, and Billy knew it, but he at least appreciated that his mate had made an effort.

'All right Dave, don't worry about it but I hope you don't fucking snore.'

Chapter Six

Wednesday 22nd August, 1979

Chris drove his scooter as slowly down Brixton Hill as he could, despite the cars that were almost touching his back light behind him eager to get past. He had only passed through Brixton a few times and it was another country as far as he was concerned. There were more than a few geezers lurking in doorways and scowling at him as he drove past but the sense of unease he had lurking deep in his stomach was tempered with the surge of excitement he felt over seeing Charlotte again. Finally, just the two of them tonight without her moody friends dragging her away and his mates dragging him into yet another punch-up.

He was pulled up at a set of traffic lights close to the tube station when he noticed Charlotte strutting confidently down the street. His heart soared and his stomach tightened, she was looking fantastic. Underneath her olive pilot jacket her light blue checked trim-fit shirt was tightly restraining her shapely bosom and her plain black mini skirt revealed those shapely fishnet-clad legs once again. For some reason it was the crisp, white ankle socks and gleaming loafers that turned him on the most, so much so that he felt that maybe he was a bit of a perv. He had read something about shoe fetishists in a copy of Men Only that someone had stashed in one of the cubicles at his work. Whatever the explanation – one thing was for sure – he wanted to poger the granny out of it.

'Get a move on you dozy bastard,' someone in a white van behind him yelled as a few other motorists parped their horns in frustration. Chris looked up and noticed the lights were green. He jolted his scooter forward and looked ahead for the next available parking space. He was almost at the club before he could find a spot to pull up. As he wrapped a heavy chain between the wheels of his PX he saw Charlotte strutting towards him unaware of his presence. A few geezers lurking in a doorway shouted something rude at her as she passed them but she just threw back her head and laughed loudly as she raised her middle finger into the air. Then she noticed Chris at the roadside and strolled over.

'So we meet once again Mr Glory Boy,' she said as she leaned over the scooter and gave him a peck on the cheek. 'Are you ready for a night of real music?'

Chris smiled awkwardly, he could never work out whether Charlotte was being playful or taking the piss.

'Yeah, I'm up for it.'

'Well let's go then,' she said as she grabbed him by the arm and half dragged, half led him down the road. They had barely walked a few yards before Chris noticed three skinheads hanging around a doorway close to the club passing around a bottle of sherry. Not the good stuff favoured by the toffs though but cheap tramp juice. He steeled himself for some kind of confrontation and a real resentment boiled up quickly inside him. Did it have to be this kind of bollocks every night?

'All right darling,' parped one of the boneheads.

'Fuck off,' said Charlotte and they continued walking but the tallest of the trio leapt in front of them.

'Where you off to? You're not going in there are you?' he said as he jerked his thumb towards The Ace.

'Yes we are, if it's any of your fucking business,' said Charlotte witheringly.

The guy stared at Chris.

'What's up with him? Is he a fucking mute?'

Chris said nothing but he felt his rage grow. Every night. Every fucking night it had to be this. Confrontation. Grease, hooligans, skinheads, punks even the Welsh. Everyone at each other's throats. Fuck it. If that was the way it was going to be fuck it. Charlotte would probably drop him like a hot potato but he was past caring. He was a Mod and if all the cunts that did not like that wanted to have a go then they could get in line. That was obviously just how it was going to be.

'What the fuck are you doing going in there mate,' continued the geezer. 'It's full of darkies.'

'Are you fucking thick or what?' spat Chris, he could not believe the shit he was hearing, and in this part of town as well. 'Where do you think skinheads came from? Their whole fucking culture came from the West Indians. This is what they were listening to, not the fucking racket you dickheads listen to. You're not skinheads. You are fucking bald punks. An embarrassment. Real skinheads wouldn't fucking think twice about kicking you up and down the street.'

The skinhead looked confused and, struggling to find an answer, he leant on a few old favourites to keep him going.

'White is right mate,' he rambled. 'These darkies are taking over. There ain't no black in the Union Jack.'

'Yeah? There ain't no red, white and blue people walking around either, mate.'

Chris steeled himself for the first blow but a couple of the bouncers from The Ace had heard the racket and started to move over to see what was happening. The shaven threesome moved a few steps back and started to unleash a torrent of insults upon Chris and Charlotte as they walked away.

'You're a fucking disgrace to the white man,' yelled the tallest geezer.

Chris stood still and stared at them while breathing heavily. He wanted to both run away from them and run at them at the same time. Charlotte gave his arm a squeeze and pulled him towards the club. Her words soothed him almost immediately and he noticed that she was smiling.

The Ace was a huge building that had once been an Edwardian cinema but was now stripped of all its glory. Once they had made it past the glowering bouncers, they stepped into its cavernous interior and onto its sticky carpets. Chris was surprised to see so many folks in this big hall just to listen to records, as usually this was a live music venue. Even so, it was midweek and there were still huge patches of punter-free space across the room. They got served at the bar quickly then managed to find a small table close by and sat down. Charlotte took off her pilot jacket and laid it down beside her. Chris surreptitiously clocked her shapely body once more and felt a ripple of excitement run through him.

'So do you come here often,' said Chris then immediately realised he had unleashed the corniest of all chat up lines.

Charlotte laughed.

'Are you fucking joking or what?'

'I didn't mean it like that,' said Chris as his face reddened. 'I meant do you come here? To Brixton?'

'Yeah,' she replied. 'I sometimes come here to buy records or I come to this club night. The people are very friendly.'

I bet they are, thought Chris. Friendly enough to a good looking bird. He wondered how long he and his mates would last down here once Dave got his hammer swinging.

'So do you and your friends come to this club?'

'Sometimes,' said Charlotte. 'Sometimes it's just me. I always meet people.'

'What, other guys?' said Chris. He knew he sounded jealous but he just could not hold the question back.

Charlotte looked at him questioningly.

'Yeah, some guys, some girls. Whoever is about.' As if to prove her point she gave a friendly wave to a trio of young Jamaican geezers who were standing at the bar and looking over. 'Anyway, I'm here with you now. What have you been up to this week?'

'I was at the Bridge on Monday,' Chris said. 'I thought you might be there.'

'I had college work to do,' said Charlotte wrinkling her nose, 'And I didn't fancy Small Hours very much, they are a bit too like Springsteen.'

Chris had thoroughly enjoyed the gig but he kept his opinion to himself, he also kept quiet about the bar room brawl at the Wellington.

'It was a good night,' he said. 'Fucking packed. Things are really happening down there.'

'Yeah, all you Mods are multiplying like bacteria,' Charlotte said with a laugh. 'Once Quadrophenia comes out it will be unstoppable.'

Chris's mood darkened and he took a deep drink from his lager.

'That will fucking kill it,' he growled. 'All sorts of plastics and bandwagon jumpers will get on board. There are even some punks in the film, bleedin' Toyah Wilcox and that blonde haired tit from The Police. Fuckin' Sting, he sings like he's been stung alright.'

'You can't keep it all between you and your mates at the Bridge House and The Wellington,' said Charlotte. 'If the bands are good they've got to get about. It's not just happening in London. Look at The Jam, they are touring all over the world.'

'I know that but this is different. The bands around our scene are just geezers like us. We've seen them in skanky pubs and clubs when there has only been us and a few regulars watching.'

'Things change Chris. You've just got to enjoy what's happening now. Nothing lasts these days.' She paused and added. 'Nothing ever did. Life moves on, like a river. Mod was all about change.'

Chris felt disappointed and a little angry at the way she seemed to be casting off his lifestyle as a passing phase. Right now he couldn't see anything beyond being a Mod but deep down he felt that there was a grain of truth in what she was saying. When he had been at school there had been a couple of older geezers who had been punks back in 1976. They had been the first punks he had ever seen on the streets around his patch and they looked fucking amazing in their boots, bikers' jackets, skin-tight denims, and ripped t-shirts. They were real celebrities around his school and always pulling loads of birds. It was the first time that he had ever realised that you don't just have to be like everyone else and that standing out from the crowd was not a bad thing. He had seen them the other day though and they were both wearing all black clobber and what looked like a bit of eyeliner. They had cropped their hair and dyed it blonde like that geezer from Tubeway Army. That was not even music, just some fucking bleeps from a computer.

Charlotte noticed that Chris had drifted off and gave him a gentle dig in the ribs.

'Are you all right?' she smiled. 'Not boring you am I?'

Chris snapped back out of his daydream

'Eh, no. Sorry, I was just...'

'I'm not having a go Chris, it's just things change so quickly these days. You've just got to live in the moment and enjoy what's happening now.'

She stood up and grabbed his hand.

'And right now my favourite song is being played so move your arse.'

The DJ had slipped on Symarip's Skinhead Girl and it was rattling out of the sound system as Charlotte dragged Chris onto the dance floor.

Charlotte loved what they played at the Ace, all original Ska and bluebeat belting out of towering home-made speaker cabinets the way it was intended, and she kept Chris on the dancefloor for most of the night. In between that they chatted and laughed almost constantly but deep inside Chris still did not know how the evening would end. He longed to get a firm grip on her but maybe she was just one of those girls that wanted to be a mate. Either way she was great company and the evening flew by before Charlotte said she had to go before midnight.

They stepped out into the street and the place was still buzzing like a Saturday afternoon. As they walked up the road towards the tube Charlotte grabbed Chris by the arm once more. They reached Chris's scooter first and he was relieved to see that it was still in one piece, although someone had stuck a flyer for a New Wave night on his fly-shield.

'Would you like me to give you a lift home?' said Chris. 'I've got a spare helmet.'

'Always got a helmet handy in case you pick up a bird have you?' said Charlotte with a wicked smile.

'No, I...' said Chris then cursed himself silently. He was stuttering like a fucking idiot. Normally he could lay on the chat with the crumpet smooth as you like but with Charlotte it was different, he was always on the back foot.

'All right, all right, don't sweat it,' she giggled. 'Yes kind sir, you can drive me home. It's up west though. Can you handle it?'

'No problem,' said Chris trying to hide his elation. Charlotte jumped on the scooter with Chris and strapped on the helmet.

'Don't you go revving up too quickly just so that I grip you tighter you dirty bastard,' she whispered gently in Chris's ear. Chris beamed and before he hit second gear he already had a full-on boner.

Chris had never been to West Finchley before and had rarely been further up North than Camden but all the way back to her house Charlotte gripped him tightly and yelled directions over the buzz of the Vespa's engine and the rattle of its fucked exhaust. As they got closer to her house, Chris realised he was smack bang in the heart of suburbia. The gardens here contained finely trimmed hedges and shapely rose bushes, not the selection of empty beer cans, old sofas and discarded porn mags that filled the meagre green spaces around his estate. Charlotte tugged at his elbow and pointed towards a large art-deco villa that dominated the other side of the road.

They pulled up at the roadside and Charlotte looked a little embarrassed as she took off her crash helmet and passed it back to Chris.

'For fuck's sake,' he said, 'So you live around here?'

'Thanks for the lift, I must say that was very gallant of you Mr? What was your last name?' she said.

'Davis'.

'Well thank you Mr... hold up, what's your first name?'

'Chris,' he mumbled in disappointment as he pulled his scooter onto its stand and removed his helmet.

'I'm only joking,' she laughed. 'I know your name. In fact, I've been keeping a close eye on you.'

She reached out and pulled him towards her gently but firmly and kissed him. As their lips locked together, Chris could feel Charlotte's firm breasts pushing against him through his shirt. He felt his knob stiffen rapidly and he pulled his hips back slightly in case she thought he was rubbing himself off on her like a randy mongrel. That didn't stop him sliding his hands down her back until they rested on the thick material of her mini-skirt. He squeezed gently and shivered with pleasure as his fingers discovered her firm bum cheeks. After a few more minutes of warm, wet kissing and arse fondling, Chris's probing fingers fumbled deeper below the hemline. Charlotte was onto him like a shot. She stopped kissing and slapped his hand away sharply.

'If you think I'm getting poked outside my house with my dad twitching behind the curtains you've got another thing coming,' she said with a wicked grin. Although they were still locked in an embrace, Chris looked a little shocked and unsure what to do next.

'I didn't say stop kissing though,' said Charlotte softly and they both locked lips once again. Before long their lips were raw and Charlotte pulled away gently.

'My old man's probably loading up his shotgun in there. I'd better go,' she said as she planted a final kiss on his cheek and started to walk up the long front path to her house.

'Will I see you later then,' said Chris, a little louder than he actually expected.

'You might Mod boy, you might,' she said as she flashed a mischievous smile.

Chris felt a dull thud in his stomach as Charlotte gave him a wave and disappeared into her house. As he kicked his PX back to life he giggled to himself. If the lads knew how he was feeling now he'd be fucked.

Chris rode all the way back home on a high. Even the traffic lights seemed to be going his way as he rode past one green light after another. That kiss with Charlotte had elated him and all he could think about was how their relationship would progress. He wanted to hold her tightly again, spend more time with her and obviously the allure of sweet, sweet sex was now on the horizon. It was overwhelming and, as his imagination moved into overdrive, he left just enough attention on the road to get home in one piece.

He was not watching the streets too closely though and failed to notice the Morgan boys marauding urban commando unit who were stalking the streets. The brothers, Monkey Harris and two other boneheads had made their way east for some midweek vengeance, still smarting from their tussle outside the Wellington. Their turf. It had been a fucking liberty. Not one of them could focus on anything else other than revenge. They wanted Mod blood, preferably that of Chris and his mates, but they were not that fussed. Anyone would do.

When they saw Chris on his Vespa, idling at a red light, they thought all their Christmas's had come at once. They moved towards him as one and as the light turned amber Barry Morgan picked up a metal newspaper advertising board and hurled it at the scooter's front wheel. Before Chris could work out what was happening, his scooter was on its side in the middle of the road and he was attempting to crawl onto the path under a hail of heavy kicks. Boot after boot dug into his stomach, back and legs. He could barely breathe as each gasp of air he took was expelled by another thudding kick. His attacker's shouts seemed muffled and distant but one piercing cry filtered through the racket and filled him with fear.

'Get his fucking helmet off, I want to cut him,' shrieked Monkey Harris.

Hands began fumbling for his chinstrap but Chris fought back with a fury, kicking out wildly while struggling to keep his hands over the open face of the helmet. There were too many of them though and gradually each limb was pinned to the ground and, as his helmet was plucked from his head, he could see five leering faces staring down at him and Monkey's Stanley blade glinting under the streetlights. Chris was gripped with fear. A good old punch-up was fair enough but this was something else. He closed his eyes tightly and waited for the stinging blade to make its mark.

'Wagwan,' a voice shouted out behind him. 'What ya skinny heads up to. Leave the bwoy alone.'

Close to where Chris was lying was an old shop unit with boarded up windows. It was brightly painted but only a select clientele ever found out what was on offer inside. Eight towering Rastas had emerged from the shop to investigate the racket and they were now lined up close to where Chris was being beaten.

'Fuck off sambo,' shouted one of the Morgan's caveman associates. The Rasta that had shouted was holding some kind of long, ceremonial wooden staff and with a mere flick of his wrist he whacked the skinhead across the forehead with it. The force of the blow created a heavy gash and the caveman fell to the ground instantly in a crumpled heap. The Morgan boys leapt to their feet just as the Rasta struck again with lightning speed, slamming the heavy weapon down on Monkey's knee. The whining sadist dropped his blade as he instinctively gripped his shattered knee-cap. Nobody moved but the Morgan boys' mob looked decidedly whiter than before.

'Now go,' commanded the Rasta. 'Leave this place with your wickedness.'

Mark and Barry Morgan looked at each other. Backing down from this tribe was degrading but this was Bruce Lee shit. Monkey and the caveman were fucked and the other seven Rastas looked as game as the first guy.

'All right Sambo,' spat Mark as he helped pull his stricken mates to their feet, 'But we'll be back.'

'I'm sure you will snowflake,' laughed the Rasta. 'I'm sure you will. Now be gone you blad clart.'

Monkey Harris was in agony but he still had enough energy for a final idle threat towards Chris.

'And we're not finished with you yet you mod cunt.'

Chris was still flat on his back, staring at the stars, struggling to force some air back into his lungs but glad that Monkey's blade had not met its intended target.

'Rise up brother,' said the Rasta as he held a huge hand out and pulled Chris onto his feet.

'Thanks,' was all Chris could mumble.

'The enemy of my enemy is my friend,' boomed the Rasta as he gave Chris a friendly slap on the back. 'Go in peace brother.'

Chris smirked a little as he picked up his helmet and lifted his scooter back up. These geezers were like fucking preachers. He had gone from the warm buzz of romance to extreme violence then religious sermonising in just a few minutes. As he kicked his Vespa back to life he noticed that the turn off to Canning Town was just a few yards down the road. What a fucking night! What the lord gives in one hand he takes away with the other.

Chapter Seven

Friday 24th August, 1979

Chris, Billy and Dave emerged from West Hampstead Underground into the night and immediately lit up their fags. They all stood silently for a few moments watching the punters that buzzed around the entrance to the station. All three of them were suited and booted for a night out and they stood out starkly amongst the throng of mostly half-pissed office workers who were heading home to suburbia after a few drinks after work. Chris sneered and hoped he would never become one of them, faceless drones whose only thrill was an office party or chicken-in-a-basket with the wife at a tennis or golf club social.

'Where the fuck is she?' said Dave moodily.

'For fuck's sake we've just arrived,' said Chris. 'She will be here.'

'I don't know mate,' said Billy. 'You are not setting a good standard here. Chasing after a bird you have only just met and dragging your mates along. You're giving her the wrong message. She will take the piss, I'm telling you.'

'Piss off,' was all Chris could manage in reply but he was feeling slightly uneasy. He could almost still feel the warm glow he got from that kiss with Charlotte and when she had phoned him this morning and asked him if he wanted to go and see a band he had jumped at the opportunity – even though it was The Members. Now standing here with his two mates reluctantly in tow he was not so sure he had made the right decision. Billy certainly was not.

'You should have waited a few days mate. Keep them keen. God almighty what did you get off her last night? It must have been good.'

'He probably got fuck all,' sneered Dave as he flicked his dog-end onto the road. 'A fucking love bite on her doorstep and a kicking from those Morgan twats.'

'That could have happened anytime,' said Chris. 'They were on our patch looking for a return match after last Friday.'

'Baldy cunts,' spat Dave. 'I'll give them a fucking return match next time I see them.'

Silence descended on the trio once again and Chris felt an air of gloom descend on him. Neither Billy nor Dave seemed in a particularly good mood and Charlotte's non-appearance was not helping.

'This had better be worth it mate,' said Billy. 'You should at least be getting some poking out of this.'

'Who's getting some poking?' said Charlotte as she suddenly appeared behind them.

Chris went bright red and started stuttering like an oaf.

'Charlotte. How are you doing? We are just waiting for you.'

'Yeah,' she smiled wickedly. 'I can see that. Well I'm here now.'

'This is Billy and Dave. My mates,' said Chris, struggling to regain his composure.

'I've seen these two before. Many times. Evening,' she said brightly.

Both Billy and Dave grunted in reply. Charlotte smirked, she had them where she wanted them already. She grabbed Chris by the arm and moved off.

'Let's get the night started shall we. Follow me gentlemen.'

The Moonlight was no more than a cramped room underneath a boozer called The Railway in West Hampstead. The street was quiet and dark with only two fat bouncers hanging around a side door providing an indication that anything meaningful was happening. It was not a usual haunt for Dave and Billy and as the lads approached the venue Dave's loathing was clear.

'I hate this fucking place,' he spat. 'It's full of dirty cunts and glue sniffers.'

'It's all right,' said Billy. 'The Members ain't that bad and some of them punk birds are quite tasty.'

Dave jerked his thumb backwards at Chris and Charlotte who were walking a few yards behind them.

'Just because his bird barks her orders we don't all need to jump. We could have been down the Marquee watching Speedball with Gaff.'

'He's only going there to flog pills to his regulars,' said Billy as they approached the club entrance. 'If he had a cheap supply of Evo-Stik he would be here with us.'

Billy and Dave stopped to wait for Chris and Charlotte who were laughing and joking together, hand in hand.

'Look at that soppy bastard, he only met her last week,' growled Dave. 'And we have left the scooters behind. How did I get talked into this?'

Billy was starting to tire of both Dave's foul mood and Chris's lovestruck idiocy. He lit a fag and almost burnt it halfway down with a single, powerful drag.

'We left the scoots behind Mr Hughes because if you get caught drinking and driving this weekend then you are going to fuck everything up for Southend on Monday.'

Dave stared into the distance.

'I can't fucking wait,' he said quietly as he pulled the handle of his hammer halfway out of his parka pocket. 'Those fucking Teds will be getting some of this.'

'For fuck's sake,' hissed Billy. 'Keep that hidden. The bouncers are just behind you.'

'They don't give a fuck. I bet there are punters in there head to toe with spikes and studs.'

Charlotte and Chris finally caught up with the lads and both of them were grinning like newlyweds.

'All right guys?' Charlotte said breezily. 'Shall we go in?'

'Might as well, we are here now,' mumbled Dave.

Charlotte looked at Chris quizzically but he just raised his eyebrows in despair. He had seen Dave in a mood like this so many times and it seldom ended well. As they walked into the club one of the doormen shouted out a warning.

'No trouble in there tonight. Right lads?'

'Not scruffy enough are we mate,' said Billy with a grin.

'Never mind all that,' leered the bouncer. 'Just behave or you will be out on your arse.'

Dave reached into his pocket and had almost turned around when Billy pushed him further into the club.

'Not yet Dave, let us at least get a drink in first.'

The Moonlight was a real stick-to-the-floor venue that had long since seen better days. It was pretty tightly packed with a mix of pub rock fans, punks and new wave geezers in second hand suits. Generally a pretty scruffy bunch that made Dave and Billy stand out even more as they sat sullenly, close to the bar. Chris and Charlotte were close to the front of the stage and seemed to be enjoying the band although they were spending most of the time shouting in each other's ears and tentatively touching each other the way couples in the first flushes of romance do.

As Billy puffed away frantically at his fag he arched his neck to check out the crumpet while Dave nursed his pint and ground his teeth together. He had necked a few blues earlier and was pissed off as the night seemed to be going nowhere. Instead of that warm rush that he usually got, he just felt agitated and angry. The state of the place was pissing him off as well, it was dark, dirty and full of wankers. He had read in a mod fanzine the Moonlight was once known as Klook's Kleek and then the 6Ts, two places that had attracted the earliest Mod elite, and here it was now being sullied by these scruffy bastards that smelled of sweat and cider.

Dave was shocked out of his dark thoughts as one of the culprits that he had been mentally murdering banged against their table.

'Oh, sorry darling,' said the skinny punk. 'Hope I didn't knock the crease out of your trousers.'

The spiky-haired lout laughed loudly as he and his two mates headed towards the bogs. Dave said nothing but his hand reached over to the solid lump in his parka.

'Leave it mate,' said Billy as he rested a reassuring hand on Dave's arm. 'It's early doors yet.'

As the band drew their set to a close the area at the front of the venue thinned out a little. Chris and Charlotte stayed where they were; both were a little flushed from having been part of the heaving mass of bodies that had swayed and pogoed throughout the gig.

'See,' said Charlotte, 'I told you that you would enjoy it.'

'Yeah, it was all right,' said Chris with a smile.

'All right? You lying bastard,' she teased. 'You were loving it but was it not 'Mod' enough, eh? It's all just music Chris. You can like what you want.'

'I know what I like,' said Chris.

'No, you know what you should like. What the fanzines say. What your mates say, but good music is good music.'

'Oh, Yeah?' said Chris. 'So what's in your bedroom? Only a load of dusty old Jamaican 45s?'

Charlotte put her arms around Chris's neck and pulled him closer.

'Play your cards right and you might find out,' she purred. They started to kiss, lost in each other on a beer-stained carpet. In the background the DJ started to play The Merton Parkas' single You Need Wheels then he deliberately scratched the needle right across the vinyl, immediately gaining an appreciative roar from the audience.

'That's enough of that old shit,' he laughed over the microphone. 'Here's the Angelic Upstarts.'

Before the song even began all hell broke loose.

The DJ's slight was all it took to push Dave over the edge. The whole evening had been winding him up tighter and tighter. The shit music, the endless glaring that was focused on them, Chris's soppy antics... it was all too much. He kicked over the table so violently that three people close to the bar got whacked with a shower of beer glasses and formica. With impeccably bad timing, the geezer that had bumped into Dave and Billy's table on the way into the bogs was just coming back out as Dave freed the hammer from his parka. The hefty thud of metal on bone shattered the bridge of the punk's nose and he dropped to the floor like a sack of potatoes. Dave swung his hammer again, catching his victim's friend on the shoulder with a crack. A huge crowd surged towards Billy and Dave, mostly punks who sensed an easy target and fancied a nice bit of pummelling to finish the evening off. Billy tried to ward them off by hurling a few bar stools into their midst but soon the regulars were upon them from every direction. Thankfully so many people were trying to take a pop at the same time that they were getting in each other's way.

Chris had his arm around Charlotte and was trying to guide her towards the door when a bearded student type reached through the melee and slapped her hard on the back of the head.

'Fascist bitch,' he whined.

Chris immediately grabbed the guy by the lapels and forced his hairy mug down onto his knee. The student yelped and fell back under a table where he remained, temporarily blinded by blood and broken spectacle glass while trying to fight off Chris's vicious kicks.

Within seconds people were almost queuing up to take a slap at the Mods and Chris and Charlotte pushed through the gauntlet of fists and boots. Chris was almost relieved when a brawny pair of arms gripped him from behind and bundled him down the stairs into the cold, fresh air. The bouncer heaved Chris out of the door and he slammed against a parked car. The contact winded him badly and he was dazed for a few moments. He felt someone kick him up the arse then heard the club door slam shut. As his mind came back into focus he noticed Dave and Billy a few yards up the street and he staggered towards them.

'Look at my fucking suit,' fumed Dave. 'Those fucking soap dodgers. This ain't over.'

'Where's Charlotte?' said Chris as he wiped a single drip of blood from his nose.

'She's fucked off,' said Billy. 'For a Skinhead bird she ain't got much of an appetite for bovver.'

Chris dusted himself off as much as he could.

'I'd better go and find her.'

'You what?' growled Dave. 'It's round two coming up mate. Those fucking punks are taking liberties.'

Chris said nothing but shifted uncomfortably on his feet. Billy could see that his mate was not in the mood for more violence.

'You go and get her Chris,' he said. 'He's no use to us anyway Dave. Don't want him tripping over his hard on when we get those bastards.'

'Do what the fuck you want then,' grunted Dave then he nodded at Billy. 'C'mon then, let's get tooled up.'

Dave stomped off towards a row of condemned shops and, as Billy followed him, he turned and gave Chris the thumbs up.

'Give her one for me mate,' he shouted.

Chris stood alone for a moment. He felt bad. The battering he had taken from the punks was nothing. His mates were off on a kamikaze mission without him and here he was about to chase after some bird he had only met a week ago. They needed his help and they had watched his back so many times. To be fair, they had also dragged him into a few scuffles as well. Only this week he had been trading blows with Wrexham thugs, Millwall mugs, punks and the Morgans. Even his bruises had bruises but the dull ache that he got in his stomach when he thought of Charlotte hurt much more. With one more quick look over to where Dave and Billy had gone he set off to find her.

Dave's heavy kick opened the door of the boarded-up shop with a crack. The stale smell of the interior repelled Billy.

'It fucking stinks of piss in here,' he protested.

Dave gave him a heavy shove into the building.

'Get in you ponce.'

A distant chink of streetlight was all that illuminated the crumbling store. What remained of the counters and display units had been vandalised and beer cans and god knows what else were strewn across the floor.

'I'm fucking sticking to something here,' moaned Billy. 'Remind me why we are pissing about in this old shit hole will you?'

'Getting tooled up,' hissed Dave. 'Those fucking punks were taking liberties and the bouncers were backing them up. Cunts.'

'They've probably fucked off by now,' said Billy.

'We'll find them,' said Dave quietly as he peered into the darkness for a suitable weapon.

'Can't we just use something from your extensive hammer collection,' mocked Billy

In his rage, Dave completely missed the sarcastic tone.

'I must have dropped it inside The Moonlight. Now come on, get yourself sorted out.'

'What with?' said Billy. 'Old beer cans? There is nothing but shit about.'

'There's a sink over there. Get some piping.'

'Great,' sneered Billy. 'If the old bill catch us in here they'll think we are a couple of pikeys after the scrap.'

'Stop fucking moaning,' yelled Dave. 'You're like an old woman.'

'Well I've spent better Friday nights. A kicking outside a punk gig and now hanging around a fucking wino's social club with you. At least Chris had the sense to piss off and get his end away. Why can't you just leave it?'

''Cause I can't,' screamed Dave with a fury that stunned Billy into silence. Dave scanned the room frantically for a makeshift weapon and finally found a small table with long sturdy legs. He lifted it up and repeatedly smashed it against the wall until two of the legs fell off.

'Keep the fucking noise down,' hissed Billy.

Dave handed Billy one of the broken legs. Two three-inch screws protruded sharply from the top.

'Right, let's go.'

'Wait a minute,' said Billy. 'Give me a chance to knock the screws out.'

'Leave them in,' said Dave darkly. 'They fucking deserve it.'

Charlotte was stomping down West End Lane when Chris finally caught up with her. She could hear him shouting her name but ignored him. He finally got close enough to grab her arm.

'Get the fuck off of me,' she yelled.

'Charlotte, please, hold on,'

'No, fuck off,' she said as she kept on walking.

'Please. I'm sorry,' pleaded Chris.

Charlotte stopped and spun round to face him. Her eyes were blazing and her face was tinged with red. Chris felt a little nervous, and a little turned on.

'What the fuck is wrong with you,' she shouted. 'I've only known you for a week and every time I have met you you are either in a fight, about to fight or recovering from a fight. What are you? A fucking psychopath?'

'No,' Chris blurted out, 'That's not me. It's just been a bad week. I... my mates just...'

'Your mates made you do it?' she interrupted. 'Fuck off. What are you? Ten?'

A middle aged couple across the street had stopped to gape but Charlotte gave them a double-barrel of expletives that sent them on their way. Once again Chris shuffled on his feet in silence. Charlotte sighed but did not walk away.

'Charlotte, please,' said Chris as he touched her hand. 'It's just been a bad week.'

She shook off his touch and crossed her arms.

'I don't know Chris. This isn't going too well. Those mates of yours... they are nice enough guys but I know their type. They are always going to be fighting. I thought you were different.'

'I am different,' said Chris then immediately cursed himself at how unconvincing he had sounded.

Charlotte let out a deep sigh and looked thoroughly pissed off. She stared at Chris and they stood in silence for a moment but slowly she began to lighten up.

'Soppy bastard,' she said with a smirk.

Chris felt a surge of relief.

'You believe me then,' he said smiling.

'No I don't,' she said as she gave his hand a squeeze. 'You're just another Canning Town yob but I think you have got something a little bit different.'

'What is that?' said Chris as they started to embrace. 'Charm? Good aftershave?'

'No,' Charlotte said as her firm, warm breasts pressed against his chest. 'You're a persistent bastard.'

As they kissed deeply, Chris felt any nagging guilt from leaving his mates behind drift away and it was replaced with a wonderful warm glow all over and an immediate stiffening in his Hampton Wick.

Dave and Billy walked down the dark streets close to the Moonlight at a determined pace. Just around the corner from the club Dave gestured to Billy to slow down. Billy was a little worried. He liked a scrap as much as the next man but Dave was treating this like a raid on an Embassy. He always seemed to take it too far, almost relishing the violence. For Billy, if it was a toss-up between a punch-up or a knee trembler he would always choose the latter but Dave seemed driven to confrontation. Everywhere they went Dave was sizing up the place for potential adversaries rather than checking out the crumpet.

Dave poked his head around the street corner and saw that the street was empty apart from two bouncers. He gestured to Billy to look for himself. The doormen were a right pair of lumps. Thick necks, beefy moustaches and ridiculously permed barnets that rested just above their shoulders.

'There's no one about,' said Billy quietly, 'The punks must have fucked off. Never mind eh?'

As Billy tried to walk away Dave gripped his shoulder firmly.

'Those two cunts are still there. They had a go as well.'

'Come on Dave,' protested Billy. 'Two skinny Mods against those shithouses. It's over mate.'

Dave took in a sharp breath and visibly seethed.

'Fine, I'll get them myself.'

'Fuck off Dave, that's suicide.'

'Look at your suit,' spat Dave. 'Look at your Fred Perry. Fucked. Just because of some Hampstead punks and their bouncer mates. It's out of order Bill and we've got to sort it. All right?'

'All right,' said Billy quietly.

Dave slapped him on the shoulder hard.

'All right mate. Let's fucking do it.'

Apart from dealing with a few rowdy Mods, it had been a quiet night for the bouncers at the Moonlight. Only the bands and their hangers on remained inside and the best they could hope for was a stray bit of skirt to come along that was in the mood for some beefcake. They chatted quietly to each other while taking every opportunity to flex their muscle-bound arms and suck in their beer guts.

They were so relaxed that Dave and Billy were almost upon them before they noticed. One managed to squeeze out a quip about 'the Small Faces' before Dave struck him across the face with the table leg. The sharp screw poking from the woodwork cut the bouncers face from ear to top lip and the skin peeled apart grotesquely. As he lifted both hands to the gaping wound, Dave swung the stick once again, striking the bouncer on the shoulder and letting the metal spike dig into flesh once again.

Billy was not so lucky. His swing at the other bouncer was dodged easily and he was knocked to the ground by a single sovereign-ringed fist to his jaw. As Billy dropped to the ground his weapon clattered to the pavement and the bouncer followed through with a hefty stamp to his nuts.

Dave's foe had recovered surprisingly quickly and he rushed forward, head down. Dave tried to take another swing but the bouncer crashed into him and sent him flying into the windscreen of a parked car.

'Oi, that's my fucking car,' came a yell from the background.

A small crowd from inside the club had come outside to investigate the racket and they looked pissed off. Even Dave sometimes knew when it was time to go and he rolled off the shattered windscreen and across the bonnet of the car back onto his feet. Billy could barely move, his body wracked by pain and nausea but Dave dragged him to his feet. As they hobbled down the road, taunts and empty beer glasses rained down behind them.

Chris and Charlotte had been kissing and cuddling in the top deck of the bus all the way back to her patch at West Finchley. Some of the petting was getting increasingly heavy but Charlotte suddenly broke away sharply and frantically rubbed the steamed-up window by their seat.

'It's my stop,' she gasped and broke away from his amorous clutches. 'Let's go.'

Chris was a little dazed as they leapt off the bus and he found himself in semi-detached suburbia for the second time that week. He wondered if he would make it past the front door this time or was he going to be waddling down the street with blue balls once again. Charlotte's house was shrouded in darkness, illuminated only by a single street light.

'Have you spent that much on the house that you can't afford electricity,' joked Chris.

'Cheeky bastard,' said Charlotte. 'There's nobody in. My mum and dad have gone to a concert.'

'A concert? What, like a band?' Chris found this inconceivable. The most his folks ever went to was a cabaret night at the social. Their idea of a good night out was watching some fat bastard in a tuxedo wail in the background as they munched down chicken in a basket.

'They went to see something at the Royal Festival Hall,' said Charlotte.

Chris knew where that was, he looked at it every day from the upper floors of the Shell Building. Some of the managers went there regularly and they were a right bunch of ponces.

As soon as Charlotte welcomed him into the house, Chris's mind immediately snapped back from venomous thoughts of his employers to the matter in hand. Here he was at the house of a girl he had drooled over for so long. Her parents were out and she had still invited him back. They were alone at last and the very thought made his knob stiffen like a poker. He felt self-conscious in case it was clearly visible through his Sta-Prest trousers.

'Go and sit in the lounge and I will get us some drinks.' Charlotte pointed into a large room at the front of the house then made her way into the kitchen.

'And take your shoes off,' she yelled from the other room.

Chris did as he was told and walked slowly into the room as he felt along the wall for a light switch. A large chandelier illuminated the room and the whole place was unlike any gaff he had seen before. All of the furniture was old but well maintained, probably antique, but the most striking feature was almost an entire wall of packed bookshelves. A small television sat in the corner, almost as an afterthought. In his house their TV was centre stage and the only books kicking about his living room were a Sven Hassel paperback and his mum's Freemans catalogue.

He was still standing in awe when Charlotte returned with two cans of Courage Best bitter.

'Sorry, that's all we have,' she said as she handed one to Chris. 'Let's sit down.'

'When will your folks be home,' said Chris.

'They won't,' said Charlotte with a wicked gleam in her eye. 'They are making a weekend of it and staying over in a hotel.'

Chris felt an electric jolt of excitement that ran from deep in his stomach to the tip of his bell-end. They both sank into a large leather Chesterfield sofa and Chris cracked open his beer. Charlotte opened hers and sipped it gently. For a moment Chris drew his gaze from the room and focused on Charlotte. He had fancied her for ages but now he was sitting here alone with her it was making the hairs on the back of his neck stand to attention. As she crossed her legs, her tonic mini-skirt crept up her thigh and her fishnet clad legs looked even longer and shapelier. Her sky blue Fred Perry clung to her slim stomach and accentuated the firm swell of her thru'pennies. Chris's gaze moved upward to her full red lips and her soft, beautiful face which was perfectly framed by her feather cut crop.

'Excuse me,' Charlotte said sharply, rousing Chris from his stupor. 'Are you perving over me? I expect that type of ogling at the cattle market disco but not in my fucking front room.'

Chris was caught out and embarrassed. He mumbled some excuse and blushed prominently.

'You soft bastard,' Charlotte laughed. 'My big tough Glory Boy is a fucking Peeping Tom.' Charlotte put down her beer then plucked the can from Chris's hand as she leant over him.

'You don't have to look,' she whispered. 'You can feel if you want.'

Charlotte straddled across Chris and pushed his shoulders down onto the side of the couch as they kissed deeply. Her skirt rode high up to her waist and Chris squeezed her bum cheeks firmly and steadily. Her hands worked rapidly at unbuttoning his shirt until his chest was bared, then she sat back slightly and peeled off her top. She had no bra on as her breasts had a supple firmness that had no need for artificial support. Chris let his hands wander across her torso then gently stroke her budding nipples. Charlotte moaned softly then once again took control, raining warm, wet kisses down on Chris's ears, neck and body. Chris felt his member throb violently, to such an extent that he felt his y-fronts and strides could barely contain it. Charlotte obviously felt it too and she started to tug at his belt and unzip his trousers. As his old man popped up to attention Charlotte got up from the couch, looked down on him with a wicked smile, and peeled down her skirt, pants and tights in a single fluid movement. She had a wonderful body and she knew it as she saw Chris's eyes expand like saucers. Before he could pass comment she had pulled off his remaining clothes and lay down on the couch beside him.

'Have you got something,' she asked as her hand gently stroked his tight bollocks.

'Eh?' said Chris hazily as his body tingled beneath her firm fingers.

'A Johnny! Have you got one?'

'What? Oh, Yeah.' Chris reached onto the floor for his discarded trousers and pulled out a Durex that had already seen a few nights out on the town without ever being requested for duty. He fumbled to open it and the slimy chunk of latex dropped to the floor.

'Here, let me,' said Charlotte as she picked the condom off the floor, stretched it over her hand and snapped it onto his cock with an ease which made Chris wonder where she'd got so much practise. He did not wonder for long though as Charlotte straddled him once more and he felt her smooth thighs stroke against his as her moist, warm pussy slid down over his bell-end and onto the shaft of his penis. She moaned gently and rocked her hips rhythmically, pushing down on his throbber harder each time. Chris was in ecstasy but desperately trying to think of anything unsexy to keep the hare from the gate. By now Charlotte was bouncing more frantically and letting out sharp little gasps of pleasure. Luckily, her yells soon grew louder and Chris felt her warm juices flow over his balls. His body stiffened as he gripped her arse firmly and let it all go.

After some final spasms of pleasure, Charlotte moved onto her side with an arm resting across Chris's body and they bathed in a post bunk-up glow. Chris was grinning like an idiot and staring up at the ceiling, as he thought back to the events of that evening. He had abandoned his mates for this long-awaited chance to spend the most intimate of times with Charlotte. He wondered if he had done the right thing, but as Charlotte snuggled up against him he knew the answer. Too fucking right he had!

Chapter Eight

Saturday 25ᵗʰ August, 1979

'Good morning Glory Boy.'

As Chris drifted slowly out of a deep comfortable sleep he heard Charlotte's warm, soft voice in his ear. He also realised that there was a warm, soft hand cradling his ball bag and lightly stroking the shaft of his penis. He usually woke up making a tent under the bed but today his cock was getting special assistance.

'Morning,' was all Chris could say as the enormity of what had happened the night before flooded back. He pulled Charlotte towards him gently, kissed her lightly on the forehead then sank back into the large, soft pillow. Charlotte's bedroom was huge and bright. He had not noticed it last night when they had stumbled upstairs after their bunk-up on the couch. Charlotte had turned all the lights out in the house, still naked, and they had retired to her bedroom with the cans of beer. After some chat and a little drinking, they had got down to it once more for that wonderful second session that always lasts a bit longer. When they collapsed in a sweaty heap on the bed, Chris had drifted off into a cosy ecstatic kip that was miles away from the sheer exhausting blackout that he usually had at home after the bombers could keep him awake no longer.

'This is nice,' said Charlotte, her hand still resting on his semi-erect member.

'Yeah, it is,' said Chris quietly.

Charlotte removed her hand from his knob and punched him on the shoulder lightly.

'My god, you're not much of a conversationalist in the morning.'

'Sorry,' mumbled Chris. 'It's just that last night was so... wonderful.'

'What? Fighting with a load of punks at the Moonlight?' she teased.

Chris smiled and gave Charlotte a little squeeze.

'You know what I mean.'

'Oh my,' she mocked playfully. 'You have such a way with words. It's positively Shakespearian.'

'Piss off,' laughed Chris. 'How's that for Shakespeare. I've not read any of his gear anyway.'

'Not even at school?' Charlotte seemed surprisingly shocked.

'Not at our school. We heard the "right to silence" pretty often though. I was hardly there most of the time. Once I met Dave and Billy in the third year we were always bunking off.'

'Ooh, the Canning Town bad boys. Daytime crime on the streets was it.'

'It was pretty boring really. We used to just hang around each other's houses when our folks were at work. Billy's house was the best though. His big brother had a cracking record collection, loads of Punk singles we'd never heard of. He'd go mental every time he found out we had been playing them but it didn't stop us. He gave Billy a black eye once after one of us left an Angelic Upstarts single next to the radiator. That's where I first heard The Jam and The New Hearts, that's the band that became Secret Affair.'

'You really like your music, don't you?' said Charlotte. 'Even more than the football?'

Chris pulled himself up the bed a little and let Charlotte cradle under his arm.

'I can take or leave the football, that's more of Dave and Billy's thing. Oh shit, what time is it?'

'About eleven,' said Charlotte. 'Why?'

'I'm supposed to meet them down at Upton Park.'

'You're not leaving are you?' said Charlotte slightly annoyed. 'You could stay here. My folks won't be back until teatime.'

Chris was not actually sure when teatime was but it sounded tempting. He had waited so long to be with Charlotte and now here he was contemplating a day with her or yet another tear-up on the streets. Charlotte interpreted his silence as indecision and moved into a more persuasive position. She slid gently down the bed and began moving her smooth wet mouth over the rampant tip of Chris's penis. Any doubts he'd had about staying crumbled to dust as he felt Charlotte's tongue wander up and down the shaft of his cock. Fuck Dave and the rest of them... Oldham could do one.

Chris began to feel a little guilty even before he emerged from Canning Town tube station in the early evening. The time he had spent with Charlotte was beyond wonderful but he was sure there was a price to pay. He knew he had let them down and earache was obviously on the way. He did not have to wait long and as he passed the Hallsville Tavern, he heard someone banging on the window from inside. He looked over and saw Dave, Billy and Gaff gesturing to him to come in. He took a deep breath and walked into the boozer. Before the door had even closed behind him Dave was yelling.

'Where the fuck have you been?'

'Oi,' shouted the landlord from behind the bar. 'Keep a civil tongue in your head.'

Dave glowered at him but lowered his tone.

'I thought you were meeting us at Upton Park?'

'I got held up,' said Chris weakly. 'I couldn't get down from Finchley in time.'

'What the fuck were you doing up there?' said Dave.

'That's where Charlotte lives.'

'You went all the way to Finchley for a shag?' said Billy. 'You could have got one round here and saved the bus fare. You did get a shag, didn't you?'

Chris said nothing and Billy and Gaff started laughing.

'He should have a got a fuck and some green shield stamps for going that far,' giggled Gaff.

'How did it go today?' said Chris trying to change the subject.

'I'll tell you how it went,' growled Dave. 'We were still sore from the kicking we got at the Moonlight last night after you had fucked off and then we couldn't get near Oldham all day for fucking old bill. Total waste of time.'

'At least we won,' said Billy.

'It's not about that,' said Dave angrily. 'Those Northern cunts made it back home without a scratch. How is that going to look?'

No one knew the answer to that and the four of them sat drinking in silence for a bit until Chris attempted to break the ice.

'What's happening tonight? Do you fancy going to a party?'

'That might be an idea,' said Billy. 'I want to save my cash for the Lyceum and Southend.'

'Where is it?' sighed Dave.

'Stratford. It's at the house of some bloke from Charlotte's college.'

The other three groaned in unison.

'A fucking student party?' moaned Billy. 'Do me a favour.'

Should be plenty birds there,' continued Chris. 'Some free booze as well. Might be a few customers for you too Gaff.'

Gaff perked up a bit.

'You think so?' he said. 'I could be tempted Chrissy boy. Today's been a fucking washout on the retail front.'

'What do you think Dave?' said Chris.

'I don't know,' Dave answered after a pause. 'It beats going home I suppose.'

Chris took that as a general agreement and slapped the table as he stood up.

'Right, I will meet you back here in an hour. I will just nip home and get changed.'

'What's wrong with staying here for a few jars then going straight there?' said Dave.

'I, I just need to get cleaned up a bit,' stuttered Chris as he made for the door.

'His knob probably reeks of fanny juice,' sneered Billy to the others. 'Make sure you scrub the smell of pussy off that bell-end mate,' he yelled at Chris whose face beamed bright red before he could get out of the bar.

'I've warned you lot,' yelled the barman. 'Keep the fucking language down.'

'Of course sir,' mocked Billy. 'There will be no more talk of dirty cocks from me my good man.'

The three of them descended into laughter as the geezer behind the bar glared at them.

Dave, Gaff, Billy and Chris stood outside a fairly regal looking three-storey terraced house straining to hear the sounds of a party. The street was quiet and dark with no sign of life.

'Are you sure this is the place?' Gaff said to Chris who was staring at an address that was written in eyebrow pencil on a small scrap of paper. 'I can't hear nothing.'

'It's a big gaff,' said Billy. 'They could be in a back room or something.'

'147 Port Way, Stratford,' said Chris. 'That's what it says and this is where we are.'

'Check again,' said Gaff.

'For fuck's sake,' said Dave in exasperation as he pushed past them and battered his knuckles against the ornate wooden door.

Chris was wondering if inviting the lads had been a good idea when the heavy door creaked open and a young hippy with a wispy ginger beard appeared.

'Yes?' he gulped.

'We are here for the party,' Dave said in an intimidating tone.

'We are Charlotte Timms's friends,' Chris added quickly. 'She said it would be okay.'

'Oh, ok,' said the hippy. 'I'm sure that's all right then. Come in, come in.'

He clocked that they were all empty-handed.

'Eh, if you need a drink the kitchen is down the hallway,' he said. 'I'm sure there will be cans of beer or something.'

'Cheers mate,' said Gaff as he made straight for the kitchen with Billy and Dave. 'You're a diamond.'

Before the door slammed shut Chris had split from the group and was off in search of Charlotte.

Dave and Billy stood in the large kitchen draining the last cans from the solitary six-pack of lager they had found. No one else had entered the room since they had arrived and the only noise from the party was some muffled chat from the room next door and the dull beat of some progressive rock parping out of a stereo somewhere.

'I'm getting pissed off with this,' said Dave. 'This is taking a right shine off that win over Oldham. Where's Chris?'

'I ain't seen him since we got here,' said Billy. 'He is probably balls deep in that bird. Nice work if you can get it.'

'Bollocks, it's bang out of order,' said Dave. 'He dragged us to that shithouse venue last night just to please her and you and me had to take a beating while he was off muffing.'

'To be fair, I don't think hitting that geezer with a hammer helped,' reasoned Billy sarcastically.

Dave dismissed the idea with a wave of his hand.

'Fuck him. He was taking the piss. Besides, we shouldn't even have fucking been there. Why drag us along as fucking gooseberries? He barely spoke to us all night. Too busy trying to get his tongue down her throat.'

'You've got a point Dave,' said Billy grudgingly. 'I'm still sore from that tear up last night and now we are in this shithole listening to fucking Hawkwind. One goal against those Northern mugs has been the only high point of the last two days.'

Dave drained his can of lager and crushed it on the worktop with his fist.

'Chris is taking liberties Billy,' he growled.

'I think for once I have to agree with you mate,' said Billy as he opened the kitchen cupboard doors one by one and hunted down more booze. 'He is getting blinded by the snatch.' Billy slammed the last cupboard door shut. 'He is forgetting about his mates. He don't realise that we will still be here long after she has fucked off.'

'Too right,' sneered Dave. 'She's bound to fuck off to Uni or something soon and he will be left behind scratching his balls.'

Gaff walked into the kitchen with two scruffy geezers and a statuesque blond girl who was wearing a baggy jumper dress, black tights and Doc Martens. Despite her scruffy clobber, both Dave and Billy could see that she had a shapely figure lurking in there somewhere. The guys were pseudo-hippy types but their clear complexions and good dental work betrayed their roots. Dave thought about the real hippy leftovers around Canning Town with their rotten teeth and leathery skin. These two were just playing at it for a while before they cut their hair and took a job with one of 'daddy's' cronies.

'Great party, ain't it?' said Gaff breezily. 'These bleedin' students are gobbling up bombers like Smarties.'

'I hope they are paying for them,' glowered Dave.

'Oh yes they are,' said Gaff as he patted his jacket pocket. 'Although maybe we could work something out.' He winked at the girl but all her attention was on Dave.

'So you guys are into Mod, eh?' said one of the chinless wonders. 'Not bad. I really like The Who.' He launched into a tuneless attempt at the chorus of Who Are You and strummed an imaginary guitar in Townsend's trademark windmill style.

'Yeah, all right mate, don't pop a bullock,' said Billy wearily.

'I really like that type of sixties stuff too. Soft Machine, The Doors, y'know,' piped in the other hippy geezer. 'Maybe I'll get aboard the Mod train,' he said with a laugh.

Dave was not sure if the guy was taking the piss or just experiencing his first black bomber rush but either way he was pissing him off.

'You would have to get your fucking hair cut first,' he spat.

The first hippy had finished his Pete Townsend impression and obviously thought a freeform discussion was about to begin.

'But why the need for these uniforms,' he said. 'Surely it is more about the music?'

'What the fuck are you on about mate?' said Billy.

'Well Mod is an accumulation of soul, jazz, beat and more. It's a bastard genre.'

'You're a bastard,' interrupted Billy. 'It's not all about that. We've got our own thing now.'

The student ploughed on and failed to notice the growing glare in Dave's eyes.

'But you have to admit, you are only trading on what has gone before. You are revivalists attempting to...'

He did not get to finish his sentence as Dave hurtled towards him with a roar, grabbed him tightly around the neck with both hands and slammed him against the door frame.

'You don't know what the fuck you are talking about,' he hissed. 'This is our thing. We've got our own bands, our own scene and unless you are part of it, you won't have a fucking clue about what is going on.'

'Wooah, easy my friend,' said the other hippy then he immediately regretted opening his mouth.

'And you can fuck off too,' Dave screamed as white flecks of spit burst from his mouth.

Gaff laid a calming on his mate's back and tried to gently prise Dave's fingers from the hippy's throat.

'Easy mate. Come on now,' he said. 'Don't bruise the customers.'

Dave let go with a flick of his fingers and moved back to lean against the kitchen worktop once more, his face still flushed and angry. The hippy guys melted away in a flash but the girl stayed where she was. Dave glared at her.

'Aren't you fucking off as well?' he snapped.

'Why?' she asked impertinently. 'Are you going to strangle me as well?'

'I don't know,' said Dave smiling slightly. 'Are you going to talk a lot of shit about Mod as well?'

'You shouldn't hate those guys,' she continued. 'We are all facing the same struggle.'

'And what struggle is that?' said Billy.

'Against the Tories...' she began to say before Gaff interrupted.

'Fuck this. These pills won't flog themselves. I'm off.'

'Hold up,' said Billy. 'I'm bursting for a piss.'

They both left the room leaving Dave and the girl alone, eyeing each other like caged tigers.

Chris was sitting in an old easy chair with Charlotte on his lap. He noticed Gaff come back into the room and raised his hand as a greeting. Gaff saluted him then got back to business in the far end of the room where a gaggle of soap-dodgers were waving banknotes in his direction.

'It fucking stinks in here,' said Chris. 'What is that?'

'Incense,' said Charlotte. 'There is some burning next to the stereo.'

'What are we doing here?' sighed Chris. 'Shit music, shit people. It's not my idea of a good Saturday night.'

'I'm sorry Chris but I told my friend Barbara I would come. You don't mind do you? You need to take it easy anyway. It's a big night tomorrow.'

'I don't mind taking it easy but this is fucking comatose.'

'I thought you might like a little rest after today's antics,' said Charlotte as she ground her bum a little firmer onto Chris' lap.

Chris felt his cock harden once again and he slid his hand under Charlotte's tight Brutus shirt and stroked her warm, smooth back.

'You are getting me into trouble Miss Timms. Dragging my mates along to the Moonlight and this shithole. They will be thinking I'm under your spell.'

Charlotte held Chris' face gently in her hands and stared into his eyes.

'Well? Are you?'

'You never know,' said Chris with a smile. 'I just might be.'

Charlotte leaned forward and they started to kiss passionately.

'Ooft. What the fuck is going on,' said Dave as he was dragged though the darkness of the house's top floor. 'Aah, I've banged my fucking knee on something.'

'Joste's parents are converting this attic space in to a studio,' said a girl's voice in the darkness. 'They haven't got round to installing the electrics yet.'

Dave was being pulled forward blindly by the blonde girl from the kitchen. They had not been alone for long downstairs before she made it abundantly clear that she wanted more than conversation. This type of upfront approach was fairly new to Dave but not unwelcome. Most of the girls he had been with had to be coaxed out of their knickers but this one was different. After a brief kiss she demanded they take it upstairs and it was fairly clear that she was hell bent on being fucked. These posh birds let it be known what they want thought Dave. It was a refreshing change from the local girls who were struck by guilt but eventually gave into temptation anyway after a lot of persuasion, pleading and poking.

They burst into a room at the far end of the loft and at last Dave could see a little of his surroundings as a light orange glow from the streetlights outside crept in through a roof window. The room was littered with workman's tools and unfinished electrical work. A low hanging light fitting cracked across Dave's head as the girl dragged him towards a pile of dust sheets in the corner of the room. The pain on his forehead faded quickly as his desire for the statuesque hippy girl grew in anticipation.

'What did you say your name was?' said Dave as the girl threw herself down on the dustsheets.

'I didn't but if you must know, it's Melanie. Now fuck me.'

Chris and Charlotte were still kissing when Billy flopped down on the seat next to them.

'C'mon you two, give it a fucking break will you?'

The couple stopped kissing and started giggling.

'For fuck's sake, you two ain't been apart since the beginning of the week. Is this what true love looks like?'

'Maybe,' said Chris with a wicked smile just before Charlotte gave him a dig in the ribs.

'Nothing here that takes your fancy Billy?' said Charlotte.

'I'm not really into sweaty birds with hairy armpits thank you, although that sort in the kitchen was pretty tasty. I went back to look for her and her and Dave have fucked off.'

'Do you think he's getting his end away?' said Chris. Charlotte tutted loudly.

'Not likely,' said Billy. 'She's probably taken him outside for a game of croquet.

'She'll be whacking a few balls either way. Dirty cow,' sneered Charlotte.

'Oh yes?' said Chris, arching his eyebrows comically. 'Do you know her?'

'I know her reputation,' she snarled.

Billy got up from the chair and rubbed his hands together in mock anticipation.

'I might go and look for her again then.'

Gaff appeared beside them counting a large bundle of £1 and £5 bank notes.

'Right troops, let's go. The party's over.'

'We are off are we? I thought you were loving it here?' said Billy sarcastically.

'I was, until their pie and mash ran out. Some bloody hippy asked me if I wanted to 'trade' for some pills. Fuck that! I ain't walking out of here with a kaftan or a fucking mouldy old rug. Where's Dave?'

'We think he's pulled,' said Chris.

'Yeah,' said Billy. 'So we can either wait two minutes until he shoots his load or go now.'

'Fuck him,' said Gaff. 'Let's go. This party is shit and we've got the Lyceum gig tomorrow.'

'At last,' said Billy raising his arms in the air in mock praise. 'A fucking decent night out. You're a cool girl Charlotte but you ain't half dragged us to some shitholes this weekend.'

'Why thank you Billy. That is faint praise indeed,' said Charlotte with a coy smile that made Chris feel massively uneasy.

Dave had managed to peel off Melanie's dress easily and he was more than pleasantly surprised to feast his eyes upon her shapely body. Years of horse riding, healthy outdoor pursuits and good breeding had gifted her with strong thighs, a tight curvaceous tummy and pendulous but firm knockers. Wearing a bra was obviously not on the agenda and only her black tights, boots and a washed-out pair of cotton briefs were left to remove. As Dave struggled to untie her laces she had already begun to stroke her moist slice, running her smooth fingers vigorously between her legs.

'Come on,' she barked. 'Get those fucking boots off and fill me up you dirty bastard.'

So this was dirty talk. It was a new experience for Dave. With most of the girls he had been with it was lights out, tights off then silence apart from the odd moan. Dave gasped in anticipation as he tugged off her boots then started to remove his own clobber. His old man leapt to attention as it was freed from the tight grip of his Y-fronts. Dave bore down on the girl, ready to slide in to her sweet nirvana but she held him at arm's length.

'You haven't introduced yourself yet,' she said.

'I told you. My name's Dave.'

'Not to me,' she hissed. 'To pussy.'

Dave was confused but as she slowly pushed his shoulders down he got the message. Nestled between her legs Dave got to work, furiously tonguing her soaking wet Jack and Danny. He'd never gone down on a bird before but what he lacked in technique he made up for in enthusiasm. Melanie dug her heels into the grimy dust sheet and ground herself onto Dave's boat. He could barely breath but her quickening breaths and ecstatic moans were driving him on.

'Harder, lick harder you fucking oik,' she yelled.

Dave stopped for a second to work out whether this was sex talk or the snooty bitch was digging him out but when she ordered him to continue he got back to it. Fuck it. This was porn mag stuff and just like that Lady Chatterley book in the library which he had torn the dirty pages out of for wanking material.

Eventually Melanie pushed his head away roughly and flipped over onto her hands and knees.

'Give it to me... now,' she ordered.

Dave was getting a bit pissed off with her attitude but the sight of her firm, rounded buttocks and moist crack soon changed his mind.

'Do you want me to put on a Johnny?' said Dave, killing the moment a little.

'Just fuck me you fucking yob,' Melanie screamed.

Dave slid his cock in firmly, gasping with pleasure as he felt the warm, wet flesh surround his member. Melanie wailed and as each stroke thundered into her body she started to make an annoyed grunting noise as if she was struggling to unscrew the lid off a seized-up pickle jar. Dave was in ecstasy but desperate to avoid the vinegar strokes too soon. Luckily, Melanie's constant orders kept the wolf from the door as they were starting to piss him off.

'Spank my arse,' she growled.

This was a new one for Dave and he gave one of her butt-cheeks a half-hearted tap.

'Big tough guy? Hah,' she sneered. 'Harder.'

Dave slapped her firm ass once again.

'Spank me like you fucking mean it,' she yelled.

Dave had had enough and brought his open hand down hard on her smooth flesh. The slap stung his fingers and he could almost make out a red hand print on her silky, white bum.

'Yes,' she cried. 'Again.'

Dave spanked once more. Then again. With each slap Melanie's gasps grew higher and his pounding strokes sunk deeper and deeper. Melanie gave a final long, loud roar that made Dave shoot his load with a mixture of both shock and ecstasy. They both collapsed onto the dust sheets then lay on their backs sucking in one lungful of musty air after another. Dave was already thinking of how he would describe this dalliance to the guys. The trouble was, if he told them the truth they wouldn't fucking believe him.

Chapter Nine

Sunday 26th August, 1979

By the time Chris woke up it was early afternoon and the sun was streaming through a crack in his bedroom curtains. He reached onto his bedside cabinet for his watch but his fingers drifted across the ticket that was lying close to his bedside lamp. He picked it up and looked at it but his eyes were caked with sleep. He rubbed them gently and the wording on the ticket slowly came into focus. March of the Mods 1979, Lyceum, The Strand, WC2. Kick off was at 6.30 p.m., he could hardly wait. This was the big one. Secret Affair, The Purple Hearts and Back To Zero had been up and down the country all month but this was the homecoming. Bands he had seen in the pubs and clubs around London were hitting the big stage tonight. He already knew what had been growing this year and now everyone would see what had been going on. Mod was unstoppable and here was the proof, right in the heart of London. He knew Charlotte was excited about it too, not least to see Madness and The Selecter join the party, and she would be with him. He could hardly believe it. Things were moving so fast that even the beginning of the month now seemed like ancient history. He reached again for his watch and noticed it was only 1.30 p.m. He listened intently but the house was shrouded in silence. His mum and dad seemed to be out, time for a celebratory wank.

Late in the afternoon Chris emerged from bed and had a shower. He had Time For Action playing on his stereo, turned up as loud as it would go so he could still hear it in the bathroom. As he dried himself off he could feel the excitement growing steadily now. Once again his mum had come up trumps and his latest suit was pressed and hanging behind the bedroom door along with a crisp white button-down shirt. The suit even looked fucking amazing on a coat hanger. It was another made-to-measure job from Johnsons that had cost him more than his dad's entire wardrobe. The whistle was a three button dark blue job with extra thin lapels and an additional ticket pocket on the right. The crease on the strides could take your eye out. He got dressed carefully, gave his tie a final straighten in the mirror and shot out of the bedroom door buzzing with anticipation. Two minutes later he was back in the room, cursing and grabbing the Lyceum ticket from his bedside cabinet.

The whole of Saturday night had ended in a bit of a blur and when Chris had been kissing Charlotte goodnight at Stratford underground, Billy and Gaff had fucked off on the bus. He travelled home alone but he had been sure that there was some talk of meeting in the Wellington before the gig. Chris made his way there and when he squeezed in through the doors of the packed boozer he was pleased to find Dave at the bar and in a relatively good mood. Whatever had happened at the party in Stratford must have been good.

'All right Dave,' said Chris as he pushed his way through the throng.

'Chris. How you doing? The others are on their way,' said Dave. 'Get in here mate and I'll get you a beer in.' Dave shoved a few punters next to him along the bar and made a space for Chris then he shouted at the barman for two more lagers.

'So how did you get on?' said Chris.

'It was all right mate,' said Dave with a dry laugh. 'Didn't turn out so bad after all. I didn't get back to Billy's until three 'o' clock this afternoon.'

'Are you still staying at his?'

'Yeah, I'm not fucking going back home yet. My old man is still in hospital though. He got thirteen stitches.' Dave started laughing again. 'My mum told them it was a DIY accident.'

'The police didn't believe that did they?' said Chris incredulously.

Dave took another drink and sneered.

'They don't give a fuck. It's as good an excuse as any. Just another domestic to them.'

Both of them got pressed a little closer to the bar as even more punters squeezed into the pub.

'So what about that bird?' said Chris. 'Did you get much?'

'A gentleman never tells Chrissy boy, a gentleman never tells,' Dave teased. 'But I will say this, my tongue's as dry as the Sahara and my knob's still redder than the Morning Star.' He pulled down his fly and reached into it. 'Here take a look.'

Chris struggled to take a step or two back as he was never quite sure when Dave was taking the piss.

'Fuck off you bender.'

Dave laughed and did his trousers up.

'I'm only joking. Fucking hell, the state it's in, if I take it out here the pub dog will be off with it. Hold up, talking of pricks. There's Billy and Gaff over at the door. Come on drink up. We might as well head over to the Lyceum, it's fucking ridiculous in here.'

Outside the pub it was almost just as crowded as Mods spilled on to the pavement, many still clutching their drinks. Scooters were buzzing up and down the street and everyone was in high spirits.

'What the fuck is going on in there?' said Gaff. 'I'm dying for a piss.'

'It's fucking heaving mate,' said Dave. 'You've got no chance. You might as well nip round the side there and have a gypsy's up Sandell Street.'

Gaff made his way around the corner as the others laughed.

'He had better watch himself when he takes that out,' said Billy. 'I got a hand job round there once after a Chords gig.'

'Oh, Yeah,' said Dave. 'What was the geezer's name?'

Chris and Dave were pissing themselves but Billy looked peeved.

'Very funny. You are on the ball tonight Dave. It must have been a good one last night.'

'Yeah it was mate,' said Dave. 'You should try it. You couldn't pull a muscle these days.'

'I get plenty,' said Billy with a frown. 'I just don't go on about it like you two.'

Chris noticed Dave's familiar frown returning but luckily Gaff returned and lightened the mood.

'For fuck's sake,' he said loudly. 'There's fucking Mods everywhere round there as well. I had to creep right in behind a skip to get a bit of privacy.'

'Why didn't you just go to the station?' said Chris.

'Fuck off, that's where all the 'dilly boys go for their tea break. It's a bum bandit bonanza in there.'

'And you would know would you?' said Billy.

'Of course,' replied Gaff. 'Your old man told me.'

Billy punched Gaff in the arm.

'Cheeky Cunt.'

'Oi. Oi,' protested Gaff. 'Watch the fucking suit.' He straightened up his jacket and pretended to brush dust from his shoulder. 'I've got to say lads, we are all looking sharp tonight.'

'It's a special occasion isn't it,' said Chris . ' It's got to be the biggest Mod gig yet.'

'And don't forget tomorrow,' added Dave. 'That is going to be fucking huge.'

'Time for action indeed Davy boy,' said Gaff as he pulled a handful of black bombers from his trouser pocket. 'No point in the Lyceum bouncers helping themselves to this lot. Dig in chaps and let us head into town for a fine evening's entertainment.'

As they walked over Waterloo Bridge the lads were not alone as many of the punters from the Wellington were drifting over to the concert as well, along with many other gig goers. Some of the tourists and straights on the bridge seemed a little overwhelmed as a tide of smarty-dressed youths pushed past them. Chris could feel the rush of the pills kicking in along with the cool night breeze drifting off the river. It was like an army marching towards their destination. Every hundred yards or so they seemed to grow in size and when they made it onto the Strand it was overwhelming – Mods, skinheads, rude boys, curious scene sniffers and new wave punks were everywhere. All moving steadily towards the Lyceum, like a strange pilgrimage drawn towards the faded glory of this old music hall, then passing through the towering pillars at the entrance. They queued to get in as the movement of the crowd slowed to a trickle while the bouncers vigorously frisked anyone that they thought looked shady, and there were plenty. Chris looked around for Charlotte but he could see little apart from a sea of faces. As they got to the main door the bouncer gestured to Chris, Gaff and Billy to get in but he placed a hand on Dave's chest.

'Move over here mate, let's give you the once over.'

As the bouncer patted Dave down it did not take long for him to find the hammer that was jammed into his waistband. The bouncer pulled it out swiftly.

'You have got to be joking,' he smirked. 'Are you planning a bit of DIY in here? We've got geezers that do that mate. What's wrong? A Stanley knife not good enough for ya?'

The other bouncers within earshot laughed and Dave glowered at them.

'Get in,' said the bouncer pushing Dave forward gently. 'Before I change my mind.' He threw the hammer into a small pile of jackets that lay on the floor behind him. 'You can pick that up on your way out.'

Dave paused for a moment in defiance but then thought better of it and moved into the venue. Chris felt a brief rush of relief, at least they had made it through the doors without incident. Maybe tonight they could make it to the final encore without Dave fucking things up.

As they walked into the heart of the venue it was breathtaking. It was a theatre that had seen better days but it was already crammed with punters and the atmosphere was electric. Back To Zero were playing and Chris smiled. He had seen them at the Wellington once when only about forty punters appeared yet here they were on the big stage only a few months later and already a sizable crowd was gravitating towards them. Things were opening up, it was not his imagination. Here was the proof right in front of him. This was not just a gathering of East London Mods on a usual night out, this was something much bigger.

Just inside the hall were a bunch of geezers from the Barge Aground, including almost all the Glory Boys. Dave was over to them like a shot, no doubt chewing the fat over the non-event with Oldham and Gaff disappeared into the crowd to service his regular customers with the bag of blue pills he had smuggled past the bouncers in his underpants.

'Billy mate,' said Chris, 'Come with me up to the top bar. I said I'd meet Charlotte there.'

'Fuck off. You don't need me to hold your hand. You've shagged her already. Haven't you?'

'Come on, I'll buy you a beer.'

'Just bring one back,' said Billy frowning. 'I want to see the band.'

'We've seen them loads of times. Just one drink. There might be some birds with her.'

'Not those usual boilers?' said Billy grudgingly.

'No,' said Chris, 'She knows loads of folks.

Billy did not want to give in but his interest was piqued.

'All right just one but if she's not there by the time we've had a pint I'm coming back down.'

The two of them gestured to Dave that they were going for a drink but he barely noticed them. Every part of the venue was heaving but they eventually struggled to the bar and Chris was delighted to find Charlotte close by. She was standing with three Mod girls that he had not seen before. Two of them were a bit rough looking but the other was a small but very shapely girl with tightly cropped peroxide blonde hair who immediately attracted Billy's attention.

'Chris,' yelled Charlotte excitedly as she reached over and hugged him. 'This is Evvy, Tracey and Lorna,' she said as she gestured to the other girls. 'I've just met them. They've come all the way down from Glasgow, just for this.'

'All right,' said Evvy to Chris and then she turned to face Billy. 'And how are you doing?'

'All right darling,' said Billy while attempting to hide how closely he was admiring her figure beneath her tight, black mini-dress. 'I'm surprised they let you lot over the border for this.'

'Cheeky bastard,' sneered Lorna.

Evvy smiled at him coyly but stared into his eyes intently.

'I bet you're glad they did though.'

Tracey and Lorna giggled but Evvy kept staring at him.

'So what is the scene like in Glasgow?' said Chris to no one in particular.

'We are the scene,' said Evvy. 'There's a few guys kicking about as well but none of them had the balls to come down here for tonight.'

'That just leaves more birds for us then doesn't it,' joked Billy weakly.

'Aye, maybe it does,' said Evvy.

Charlotte and Chris were slipping in a little French kissing on the side when she broke off abruptly as the music kicked off again downstairs.

'Chris, that's The Selecter. We must go down,' she said excitedly.

'Sure, sure,' said Chris as he looked around the group. 'Are you coming?'

Tracey and Lorna jumped at the opportunity but both Billy and Evvy paused.

'I'm no so intae this Ska stuff, you two go down and I'll catch up with ye,' said Evvy to her friends then she turned to Billy . 'Maybe we could go outside for a fag. I've no seen much of London other than the bus station.'

'Sure,' said Billy, a bit amazed at how quickly his chat had delivered results. 'This way my dear.'

After persuading the bouncers to give them a pass out, Billy and Evvy took a walk outside. The wandered down the street a little bit and chatted. Evvy swore like a docker but she had a great sense of humour. She had a cracking pair of Bristols as well, Billy noted, and he was keen to get a little bit closer to them.

'Do you want to nip down and see the river,' he asked.

'Naw, yer alright,' said Evvy with a sneer. 'I can see the Clyde when I'm back home. Let's go doon here.' She led Billy down behind the venue where the stage gear was usually loaded in. There were a couple of roadie types lurking in the distance but Evvy pulled Billy into a doorway and they were soon exchanging tongues and locked in a warm, wet kiss. The doorway reeked of piss and old fish and chip wrappers but Billy was not bothered as he had a young blonde Modette grinding against him and it was barely eight o'clock. Evvy's rhythmic motions were really turning Billy on so he thought he would get as far as he could before she put the block on it. He ran his hands over her firm aris and gradually worked his fingers below the hemline. With still no resistance he groped further, reaching beneath her cotton briefs and warming his hands on her bare butt cheeks. She panted slightly and her tongue darted more frenziedly against his as her shapely knockers pressed against his chest. He let his fingers drift across her wet pussy lips then introduced the tip of his middle digit into her welcoming jack and danny. Evvy gasped quietly as Billy continued to probe deeper inside her velvet vice. She stopped kissing him and laid her flushed cheek against his shoulder, lifting her left leg slightly to give his hand easier access. Billy moved his fingers gently then slowly increased the strokes until he reached a frantic pace and Evvy's body shuddered with pleasure. No sooner had he removed his moist hand than Evvy began stroking the hard bulge in his trousers.

'What's happening doon here,' she laughed teasingly. 'Maybe I'd better have a look.'

She crouched down in front of him then suddenly screamed in pain. Billy nearly shit himself at the loud yelp.

'What's going on? Are you all right?'

'Some bam has left a bottle cap on the deck and I fucking knelt oan it. I'm all right.'

Billy was about to laugh loudly but Evvy soon got his attention as she wrestled his knob out through his zip and began sucking on it like a lollipop. Billy looked down as Evvy's blonde barnet moved rhythmically in the pale street light then he let go a satisfied sigh and looked up at the stars. Things did not get better than this, an experienced BJ on a warm London night, but his pleasure was soon interrupted.

'Evvy, the Purple Hearts are coming on soon. Hurry up,' came a screeching voice close by. It was Tracey, leaning against the corner of the alley and puffing a fag.

Evvy pulled Billy's member from her mouth and held it to the side of her face like a cigar.

'I'm nearly done,' she yelled up the street. 'See ye in a minute.'

'How do you know it will take a minute,' said Billy feeling slightly annoyed.

Evvy said nothing but started to gobble on his bell-end with renewed vigour. He gasped and looked up at the stars once again and then he was sure he felt a finger being jammed up his arse before a shockwave shot through his body sending his head jolting back against the brick wall and his hot seed bursting into Evvy's mouth.

'There you are,' said Evvy after spitting Billy's goo onto the pavement, 'I telt ye. Cheers.' She tidied herself up quickly and disappeared back into the venue before Billy had even done his strides up properly. He gasped for a few moments and pondered on what had just happened. He was bathed in an orange neon glow and the steady thump of music seeped through the crumbling brickwork. He felt cheap but as feeling cheap went it was still fucking good.

By the time Madness hit the stage later in the evening Charlotte was in seventh heaven and Chris noticed that a large part of the crowd were too. The response to The Purple Hearts lively set had been good but this was something else. Charlotte dragged Chris closer to the stage and soon they were deep in a sea of heaving bodies. She looked around to see if he was ok a few times but for most of the gig she was lost in the music, skanking frantically on the spot and screaming in applause after each song. Chris had heard a bit about this 2-Tone thing, they looked like Mods but this was something different, they had the place fucking leaping and it was a world away from the dusty old Ska sound he had heard on records.

As Madness drew their performance to a close Chris and Charlotte moved away from the front and found Dave, Billy and Gaff standing about halfway up the hall talking to a few of the other Monday night Bridge House regulars.

'Where have you been?' Chris asked Billy.

'I'll tell you later,' Billy replied.

'It's worth the wait mate,' laughed Gaff and even Dave smiled slightly.

'That was fucking brilliant,' said Chris. 'What did you think?'

'Not bad,' said Billy. 'Not sure about all that jumping about business though.'

'That was the best bit,' said Charlotte as she mopped her forehead with a paper hankie.

'You like jumping about getting sweaty do you?' said Billy sleazily.

'Easy mate,' said Chris with a frown.

Billy raised his hands in mock surrender.

'I didn't mean anything Chrissy. You've got a dirty mind.'

'Anyway,' said Charlotte, 'If you boys want to get down the front before your heroes come on then now is the time.'

'Might as well,' said Gaff. 'At least before it fills up with bandwagon jumpers and students.'

Dave grunted and they all moved towards the front of the stage. They had barely moved a few yards before the Morgan boys appeared before them coming the other way.

'All right darling,' one of the hangers-on shouted at Charlotte. 'What are you doing with these poofters?'

'Just kinky I suppose,' she said as she tried to keep walking. 'I've got a thing for blokes that can read and write their own name.'

'Cheeky cow,' spat Monkey Harris and a stand-off immediately began.

The Morgan boys and their mates were puffing their chests out ready for a scrap.

'Look Morgan you fucking idiot,' said Chris directly to Barry, 'Not tonight. You'll get us all thrown out.'

'I don't give a fuck,' Barry replied. 'We've seen what we came to see. I'm not hanging about for the rest of the shit.'

Even before he had finished his sentence the number of Mods surrounding him had grown as people moved forward to get closer to the stage and see what the rumpus was all about. The Morgan brothers' mob started to look decidedly uneasy. Dave stood next to Chris and stared calmly at Mark Morgan. Chris was sure it was about to kick off until Dave spoke quietly.

'Look you boneheads, there is a time and a place for this and it ain't here.'

Barry Morgan took a few steps forward until he was almost in Dave's face.

'There will be a place all right,' he growled, 'And a time but you won't know until it's too late mate.'

'Fair enough,' said Dave with a surprisingly zen-like calmness. 'See you then.'

Barry Morgan pushed past Dave and nodded for his mob to follow him. They melted into the darkness at the back of the hall.

Chris was amazed that his friend had not exploded as he usually did.

'That was nice,' said Gaff attempting to lighten the poisonous atmosphere. 'Always good to bump into some old friends.'

'Thanks mate,' Chris said to Dave quietly.

'No problem,' said Dave. 'No point in wasting a good evening.'

Chris was sure he saw Dave crack yet another rare smile but the lights were dimming for Secret Affair's appearance and he was not sure. He was not short on optimism though, a real trait he had picked up from his old mum. Maybe Dave could finally see that there were a lot better things to do than constant rucking. As his favourite band took to the huge stage Chris felt a rush that was even greater than a handful of blues. Maybe from now on every day would be as good as this one?

Chapter Ten

Monday 27th August, 1979

As Chris was roused from his peaceful sleep he could hear the tinny parp of scooter horns outside his bedroom window. He heard a muffled voice over the din.

'Get the fuck up Davis.'

He was trying to brush the sleep from his eyes when his dad burst into his bedroom.

'Will you tell those fucking herberts to keep the racket down,' he seethed. 'It's only seven in the morning. And on a Bank Holiday as well. Jesus Christ they'll have the whole neighbourhood up.'

Chris struggled out of bed and stumbled over to the window. The bright light stung his eyes as he pulled back the curtains. He could see Dave, Billy and Gaff sitting on their scooters, suited and booted already and revving their engines. He opened his window and leaned out slightly.

'Ooft. Look at that,' joked Gaff. 'Get some clothes on you pervert. Cover up that skinny white chest your blinding me.'

'What are you doing here?' said Chris. 'It's early doors yet for Southend.'

'It's never too early for that mate,' shouted Dave. 'We ain't been to bed yet. We went back to Billy's after the Lyceum and finished off those pills.'

'Keep yer voice down.' Said Chris but the rest of them just laughed manically.

'Where did you get to?' asked Billy.

'I took Charlotte for a drink after Secret Affair and when her Dad came to pick her up he brought me home as well.'

'Ooh,' said Billy in a Frankie Howard tone. 'Brought you home in the Bentley did he?'

'No, it was a Volvo.' Chris realised that sounded wank but he was too sleepy to attempt sarcasm or come up with a witty reply. His dad started yelling something from the next room.

'Look,' he shouted down, 'Piss off and I'll meet you down at Jenny's caff. I won't be long.'

'You'd better not be or we'll go without you,' said Dave and then drove off down the street. He seemed in a foul mood yet again thought Chris, obviously the bonhomie he had felt last night had long since faded.

'Don't be long Davis. No sneaking back to bed for a hand shandy,' smirked Billy and he and Gaff set off after Dave.

Chris shut the window and opened the curtains wide. It was sunny already. Surely a good sign. He scratched his balls and started thinking about what to wear.

Chris did not roll into Jenny's until about half past and eight but despite the torrent of abuse he received they did not immediately leave for Southend and sat for a while drinking coffee and trading stories of the past few days. Top of the agenda was Dave's description of his session with the Amazonian student and Billy's time with the Glaswegian horn blower. By the time they were actually ready to leave Gaff remembered he still had a stash of pills hidden under his mattress and after retrieving them from his house they found the road to the coast was already heaving with Bank Holiday fun seekers. When they finally broke free of the stifling grip of London it was past midday.

It felt good to finally be free of the city. Chris had barely seen the fields or had his scooter out of third gear all summer. As they drew closer to Southend the excitement built steadily but before they even got to the seafront there was trouble. They passed a boozer called the Five Bells which looked as if it was having a bare-knuckle boxing match in the car park. Dave gestured for them to pull over and as they brought their scooters to a halt they found a circle of skins, Glory Boys and other terrace terrors sticking the boot into a small group of Rockabillies. Chris recognised more than a few faces from their trip to Wrexham. The hapless rockers were almost spark out but that did not stop Dave from leaping over and whacking a few of them with his crash helmet. The crowd gave a little cheer for Dave's late contribution to the bovver but a couple of them eventually pulled him back. Dave was beaming with pride and he got a few congratulatory slaps on the back as Mickey Thomson and Terry Harkins had a quiet word with him. Chris could not hear what was being said but whatever it was seemed good news for Dave and he walked back towards them smiling.

'Are we going then?' said Gaff, revving his engine impatiently. 'I've got bundles of gear here that needs flogging.'

Dave ignored him, strapped his helmet back on and kicked his scooter back to life.

'What was all that about?' asked Chris.

'Nothing much,' said Dave moodily, 'But the grease down here better look out. Now let's fucking get there.'

Dave sped off out of the car park without even looking at the oncoming traffic and a cacophony of car horns greeted his surprise arrival back onto the A127. Chris, Gaff and Billy looked at each other warily but said nothing. As they pulled back onto the road Chris felt a shadow of apprehension hanging over the tingling anticipation of the day ahead.

As they got closer to Southend Chris's mixed feelings grew stronger. He was desperate to meet up with Charlotte and keen to see just how many other Mods would show their face at the seaside but he knew they would not be alone. All the way from London, vanloads of skinheads had been passing them while peeping their horns and shouting abuse. The throaty roar of motorbikes was never far away either and many bikers had roared past them flicking the Vs and making 'wanker' hand signals. When they entered the outskirts of the town the holidaymakers were out in force in the shape of old geezers in suits with just vests beneath their jackets and young families in badly fitting leisurewear, but there was a scattering of young yobs amongst them. By the time they got close to the town centre many of the ordinary holidaymakers were beating a retreat under a wave of sawdust Caesars. As they idled their scooters at the traffic lights nearest to the railway station Chris noticed that in this part of town at least, the skins were in ascendancy. They were all over the place and still streaming out of station. Every one of them looked as if they were bubbling over in anticipation of a good scrap but they seemed to be enjoying themselves at the same time. He hoped that Charlotte had made her way in from London okay and strained to see if she was around but the constantly moving flow of shaved heads around the street was too great to make out any one figure.

Billy shouted to get Chris's attention then gestured at the road behind them. Among the odd bus and taxi a huge parade of scooters stretched back as far as the eye could see. Chris beamed with pride, the Mods were obviously on their way as well. The light flicked to green and the two stroke procession continued on its way to the seafront.

After cruising around town for a bit, they soon found the spot where most folk had parked their scooters close to the seafront and they pulled up alongside them. Dave immediately started looking around for even a sniff of oil-stained denim and the rest of them took off their helmets and gloves and sorted themselves out. Charlotte must have been waiting there because as soon as Chris pulled his helmet off a smooth pair of hands reached from behind and covered his eyes.

'Guess who?' she squealed excitedly.

Chris turned around quickly and lifted her off the ground with a hug.

'Are you ok? I saw loads of skins outside the train station.'

'Well they are not going to bother me are they?' she shrieked happily and planted a squelching smooch right on his lips.

'All right you two,' laughed Gaff. 'Take it easy. We're here for a look about, not a dirty weekend in a bed and bunk-up.'

They wandered around for a little bit but it soon became evident that all the Mods and skins were gravitating towards the beach and the mob was growing larger by the minute. With Charlotte on his arm, his mates by his side and a crowd of like-minded punters around him Chris felt like an emperor as they strolled down the prom. He noticed a lot of Mod faces from the Bridge, the Wellington and the Barge along with hundreds more he had never seen before. No one was glaring or sneering at each other just laughing and buzzing on the atmosphere (and the pills). They all felt united and the old bill and everyone else could do nothing more than look on and stay in the background. It was like being truly unshackled for the first time. Back home they were a minority surrounded by the ordinary punters that did not understand them and the other youth cults that wanted to take a boot at them but here they were the majority. Chris knew that the feeling of power could not last but while it was there he was determined to soak it up. He squeezed Charlotte closer to him and kissed her gently on the forehead. She smiled up at him and playfully punched him in the stomach.

'Hold up,' said Dave and brought their group to a halt after a few minutes walking. 'Let's have some of them bombers Gaff.'

'Let's see some cash then folks,' said Gaff as he dug deep in his parka pocket for a small bag of pills. 'Might as well get some off you now before you blow it all on candy floss and dirty postcards.'

'Do you want some?' Chris said to Charlotte as he thrust a fiver towards Gaff.

'No you're alright,' Charlotte answered. 'I'm fine.'

Gaff dished out a portion to each of the lads and popped a few himself before he packed the remaining pills back in his pocket. They stood in silence for a moment, necking the speed and looking around at the heaving crowds.

'Why don't we go out on the pier?' said Charlotte.

'Fuck that,' spat Billy. 'It's miles long. It will be bedtime by the time we get to the end and back. That gig at Canvey Island starts at seven.'

'We could go to Adventure Island,' offered Gaff.

'Look,' said Dave angrily, 'We are not here for a fucking ride on the dodgems, we're here to do some grease and there are plenty of the cunts about.'

'Lighten up Dave for fuck's sake. You'll get your scrap. Why don't we have a little fun before we get carved up,' said Gaff sarcastically.

Dave did not pick up on Gaff's impudent tone and he had only one thing on his mind.

'Mickey Thomson and the rest of them are meeting over at the Kursaal. There's a boozer near there called The Minerva that is usually reeking with rockers. Let's head over there.'

Chris knew it had been too good to be true. There was no way Dave was going to settle for a great day out with his peers unless it ended in someone getting hurt. Usually them. Simply being there was not enough for him, only confrontation would make the day worthwhile. Chris raised his eyebrows to Charlotte and resigned himself to some form of bovver. In truth he had never expected anything else. They followed Dave who was strolling ahead as excited as a kid going for a ride on the big dipper.

The Minerva was a large two-storey boozer on the seafront, just across the road from the Kursaal amusement arcade, and it had long been known as a stronghold for Teds and Rockabillies over the years. This was grease grand central and the old bill were well aware of the fact as they had already formed a not so thin blue line around the pub holding back an army of leering skins and Mods from the two hundred or so denim and leather merchants who were using the Minerva as their Alamo. By the time Chris and his mates arrived the mob was jam packed and it had descended into a slanging match between those at the front on both sides of the divide. There were a few punches, bottles and beer glasses being thrown but the culprits were swiftly removed from the scene and launched into the back of waiting police vans, no doubt destined for a quick trip down the stairs at some Essex cop shop followed by a jailhouse breakfast. Dave managed to get in tow with Mickey Thompson who was orchestrating a breakaway group of Glory Boys that were attempting to flank the Minerva from behind in a classic pincer movement but the Police latched onto their effort sharpish and they were turned back easily. After another twenty minutes of jostling and shouting with no real end in sight Chris began to get bored.

'C'mon,' he said to Billy, Gaff and Charlotte. 'This is bollocks. There is nothing happening.'

'I have to agree with you there,' said Gaff. 'The Filth are pushing us back too far. You'd need a fucking pair of binoculars to see any grease.'

'Let's get a beer,' said Billy and they pushed out of the crowd back onto the esplanade.

Chris held Charlotte a little closer as they emerged from the mob.

'Are you okay?'

'Yeah,' she answered. 'I'm loving it.' She gave Chris a kiss and squeezed him back.

'Are you still coming to Canvey with us tonight?' he said. 'I've got a spare helmet.'

'Oh right, your "pulling some sort and taking her home" spare helmet?' Charlotte teased.

'That's the one.'

The four of them wandered past the Kursaal and up into town but each pub they passed was full to capacity with punters spilling out onto the street.

'Fucking hell,' said Billy. 'We're going to have to press on to get a beer in this town.' They wandered further away from the seafront to find an available hostelry and gradually the crowds of Mods and skins thinned out a little.

'Are you sure this is wise,' said Gaff as they kept walking past a few gift shops and greasy spoons. 'We don't want to get fucking ambushed up here.'

'Piss off,' said Billy. 'All the grease are still in that boozer and the rest have probably all fucked off back home.'

'Oh Yeah?' said Gaff pointing across the road. 'Someone forgot to tell them that.'

A few hundred yards away were a gang of greasers pushing some Mod geezer up against the wall. Chris and his mates froze to spot until they heard the Mod mouthing off at his attackers. It was Dave.

'Fucking hell,' said Billy, frantically looking around for a weapon. 'Why did it have to be him?'

'Bill, Chris, over here,' said Gaff in a hushed tone. He was standing behind a delivery van that was parked up with its back doors open. 'Take a couple of these.'

The van was loaded with crates of cheap pop in big glass bottles. Gaff passed a couple each to his mates then they all ran across the road and launched them at the rockers. Most of them smashed onto the pavement close to the gang but one met its target and hit a fat Ted square across the back of the head. As he flopped forward onto the pavement Billy screamed out.

'Dave! Leg it.'

Dave did not need persuading and he shoved passed the shocked greasers and ran towards his mates. Chris gripped Charlotte's hand and they all ran off back towards the seafront. At least they thought they were running towards the main drag but with the howling rockers in hot pursuit they got confused as they seemed to be heading deeper into the Southend backstreets. Gaff gestured towards a back alley and they all followed him.

As they ran down the narrow side street Chris prayed that it led to a main road and either the warm embrace of a mob of Mods or even a posse of old bill. Anything was better than this tribe of tattooed greaseballs getting a hold of them. The grease had been on the back foot all day but now they had a nice little bunch of Mods almost in their grasp and they were obviously itching to put their heavy boots, knuckledusters and razors to good use.

'Oh shit,' yelled Gaff as they reached the end of the alley, right into a bricked-in courtyard with a locked shutter door against one wall. They turned to face their attackers who were pounding down the alley. Chris pushed Charlotte behind him and grabbed and empty beer crate to use as a weapon. Dave already had his hammer ready and Gaff and Billy could find nothing in the dead end apart from litter. The rockers knew they had cornered their prey and walked leisurely into the courtyard. There were nine of them, all big lumps decked head to toe in jeans, bike jackets and heavy boots. They were tooled-up to a man, all wielding some form of metalwork that looked like it had already been put to good use in the past.

'All right ladies,' said the smallest but stockiest one. 'What are you running for? We just wanted to have a chat.'

'Yeah, we're from the Southend tourist board,' guffawed one of the bruisers.

'Fuck off you greasy bastard,' spat Dave. 'You want some? We are right here.'

Chris could feel the tension reach a crescendo. He reached back and squeezed Charlotte's arm. All the wonderful sensations of the day had melted away and all he could feel was a cold sick feeling in his stomach. Then he heard a sound that made his dread almost consume him.

'Oi, Canning Town poofters. We've been looking for you.'

It was the Morgan boys strolling down the alley almost ignoring the grease.

'You having a kick at these fucking Mods are you?' said Barry Morgan to the rocker at the front.

'Too fucking right,' said the greaser thinking that the skins were lining up to take a swipe alongside them as well.

'Well they're with us,' said Barry as he turned swiftly and nutted the geezer across the bridge of his nose. The greasers seemed a little shocked but the blood pouring from their mate's hooter set them off like a starting pistol. The Morgan boys started putting the boot in to which ever rocker was closest and they forced their way out of the alley pushing the grease straight towards Chris and his mates. Dave swung his hammer wildly and Chris battered the beer crate against any lairy ring-encrusted hand that was clutching a weapon. Billy managed to grab hold of a dropped bike chain and he whipped it against every rocker's skull that he could. Gaff was wrestling with a sweating thug and trying to pull his thick neck down far enough to plant a kick in his face but someone drew the blade of a flick-knife across the back of his hand and he fell back against the metal shutter with a scream.

Gaff's yell seemed to spur the skins and Mods on further and soon all of the rockers were flat out on the ground as heavy kicks pounded into them. Like a fucking parasite, Monkey Harris emerged from the shadows and slashed his blade across the cheek of one rocker who was completely unconscious.

Chris kicked the blade from Harris's grip.

'Leave him you fucking scum.'

Harris yelped in pain and cradled his sore hand. His eyes were burning with hate.

'What's it to you, you Mod cunt,' he squealed at Chris. 'He'd have done the same to you.'

'Leave it Monkey,' ordered Barry Morgan. He moved over to Chris and slapped him hard but playfully on the shoulder. 'You all right mate? You didn't think we'd let these fucking Teds do you over did you? That's our job.'

Chris thought another fight was about to erupt and then he noticed Morgan was smiling.

'I'm all right. Cheers,' was all he could say.

A Black Maria police van rattled past the entrance to the alley with its siren blaring but it kept going into the distance.

'We'd better get moving,' shouted Harry Morgan. 'I'm not going back to borstal while it's still summer.'

The Mods and skins hobbled back down the alley in various states of disrepair but Monkey Harris could not resist a final kick at one of the prone rockers who lay groaning on the blood-splattered concrete of the courtyard.

Chris thought the whole week could not get any wilder but as he sat drinking his lager, and wincing slightly as the cold liquid passed over the cut on his bottom lip, he could not believe what was happening. Here he was in a Southend boozer surrounded by Mods and skins once more and sharing a pint in the snug with the Morgan Boys. The bruises from their last meeting had barely faded yet now they were clinking beer glasses together like old mates. After leaving the courtyard scrap behind them, they had all wandered down towards the seafront avoiding any stray groups of old bill as the lot of them looked as if they were fresh from a punch-up and they did not want to give the plod an easy excuse to lift them off the street. They finally found a pub with some floor space still free and got the drinks in. Dave was sitting next to Barry and Mark Morgan exchanging war stories and Billy chatted with the rest of the Morgan mob while Charlotte wrapped a cotton hankie around the gaping wound on Gaff's hand. Only Monkey Harris refused to join the party and he stood near the bar glowering in disgust at the lot of them.

Chris laughed to himself. What had changed? What had flicked the switch between enemies and friends in such a short time? Was it just the fact that they all had a taste for a Fred Perry, a neat haircut and a Pork Pie hat or was it just because they were not 'grease'? And who were they anyway? Just another load of geezers from council estates who liked their hair a bit longer and their music a bit louder. Fucking hell, The Who were decked out in flares and long hair not so long ago. It did not make sense but in the end it was not worth bothering about. Chris knew that he was a Mod and that was what mattered. All he wanted was to look good, clean and smart and see the bands that reflected his life. Everything else would take care of itself and there was fuck all he could do about it. A loud whoop went up around the table as someone put Dave and Ansell Collins's Double Barrel on the jukebox and one of the Morgan mob got Charlotte up to dance on the tiny bit of carpet that was not covered by punters. Mark Morgan and Billy got up as well and shuffled alongside them. Chris laughed and shouted encouragement to the dancers along with the rest. What a week. Never a dull moment.

After a few more beers and a bit of dancing they all left the pub and wandered down to the seafront. It was early evening and numbers were dwindling right across town as many folks made for the train and bus stations. Even the police seemed to look a little more relaxed, although they were still mopping up isolated skirmishes across town. Gaff never let an opportunity fly past him so he had used the new entente cordiale with the Morgan boys as an excuse to flog some pills. They stopped behind a little shelter on the prom as Gaff struggled to pull the bag of bombers from his trouser pocket with his one good hand.

'Come on,' said Billy. 'Get them fucking out. It's just a cut, you ain't had your fucking hand chopped off.'

'Hold on,' said Gaff impatiently. 'I'm no good with my left hand.'

'Do you want me to get them,' said Chris.

'Fuck off, you'll probably cop a feel of my knob while you're in there. Your bird can help though.'

'No thanks,' said Charlotte with a sneer. 'His "bird" is keeping her hands to herself.'

Dave pulled out a packet of fags, jammed one in his mouth and offered the rest of them around.

'We're off to Canvey Island tonight,' he said to Barry. 'You lot coming?'

'Not on your life mate,' said Barry with a smile. 'I'm not listening to that shit again in a hurry. Last night was bad enough.'

Dave laughed and shrugged his shoulders. Gaff was still struggling to dish out the pills when suddenly there was a screech of rubber behind him. He spun around fully expecting to see a police car but it was a fucked up Vauxhall Viva with a transit van close behind it and both vehicles were full of rockers who piled out onto the street and ran towards them. Monkey Harris had been sitting on a small wall sulking slightly back from the rest of the group and two burly greasers grabbed him and dragged him kicking and screaming into the back of the van. The doors slammed shut and the transit tore off down the street with a dirty confederate flag flapping wildly from a CB radio aerial on its roof. Wherever Monkey was heading it looked as if it was going to be painful. The rest of the group turned to face the rockers but before a chain had been swung the familiar peep of a policeman's whistle cut through the tension. A group of around twenty coppers had obviously been on the lookout for any remaining trouble and they were quick to react as they pounded across the road towards the action. The rockers turned on their heels and headed back to the car. It was over without a punch being swung but Dave could not resist it. He sprinted towards the Viva, determined to do some damage despite the thin blue line that was flooding towards him. As the greaser's car engine sparked into action Dave was leaping across the bonnet like something out of Starsky & Hutch. Before the driver got his foot off the clutch, Dave took a swing through the open side window and cracked him across the skull with his hammer. The poor bastard slumped on the steering wheel and the jam-jar shuddered forward a few yards before it hit a lamppost. Dave disappeared under a mountain of blue serge.

It had been an eventful day, but seeing your mate dragged kicking and screaming into a police van was not the ending Chris had hoped for. As the coppers had descended on Dave he was struggling like a madman, his eyes were bulging and white specks of spittle and curses were flying from his mouth. He managed to land a few kicks at the police but he was no match for the burly plods who overpowered him, slapped on some handcuffs and threw him unceremoniously into the van. One of the coppers had been so close to Dave when he struck out with his weapon that some of the rocker's blood had splattered across his face. The policeman looked both disgusted and furious. Chris prayed that he was not one of the Bill that was stationed wherever Dave was being taken. The police told them and the Morgan boys to move along as they tended to the rockers inside the car and, as they went, Chris saw one of the cops put Dave's bloodied hammer in a clear evidence bag. Proof if it was needed alongside a long list of flat-footed witnesses. He did not reckon he would be seeing Dave any time soon.

They said goodbye to the Morgan boys as they got closer to the station.

'He's fucking game your mate, I'll say that for him,' was Barry Morgan's parting shot.

Not one of them had mentioned Monkey's fate as they had walked along the prom. Even though he was an evil little shit, Chris winced at what was probably happening to him now in the back of that van.

When they reached their scooters Dave's Lambretta stood there as a stark reminder of their missing friend.

'What are we going to do with this fucking thing?' asked Billy. 'He's got the keys on him.'

'We can't just leave it here,' said Gaff. 'It will be winter at least by the time he sees daylight again.'

They all had a smoke and talked things over then Charlotte had an idea and after sweet-talking a nearby shop owner she persuaded him to store the scooter in his small back yard for an unspecified time. As the steering lock was on and the wheels chained together the four of them had to manhandle the scooter across the road to its new temporary shelter.

'Are we still going to Canvey?' said Chris as they dusted themselves down.

'Too fucking right,' said Gaff. He noticed that Chris was still unsure. 'Look mate, Dave came for the bovver today and he got it. That's what he wanted. You don't bring a hammer to the seaside unless you are looking for trouble.'

'He's right Chris,' said Billy. 'I know he is our mate but he's been going fucking nuts for a few weeks now. He was bound to get lifted sometime. We can't let it spoil the rest of our weekend.'

'They're right Chris,' said Charlotte softly as she squeezed his arm and reached up to plant a kiss on his neck.

Chris looked out over the sea and the low sun was bathing it in an orange glow. He had never felt as good before as he had in these past few days but now he felt nothing. They all strapped on their crash helmets and drove out of Southend in a sombre mood.

Although they were not quite sure where they were going, as they got closer to Canvey Island they could see a fleet of scooters moving in a similar direction so they followed them and they eventually led to the Paddocks, a huge but spartan community centre that looked like a comprehensive school. The car park was already filling up with gleaming scooters and there was not a greaser in sight. Tonight the Mods were finishing up the Bank Holiday in style.

As soon as they had pulled up they were surrounded by a number of people that they knew, all recounting the events of the day. Word had somehow spread already of Dave's last stand but it had been blown up into mythical proportions. Dave now had a reputation for taking on an army of coppers single handed but none of them said anything to dispel the rumour. Once inside the hall it was obvious that many of the Mods who had been in attendance at Southend must have hit the road back home but there was still a good five hundred or so jammed into the main hall. With its plain walls, parquet flooring and small stage it resembled a school hall but the atmosphere was good and some of the buzz from the show of strength throughout the day was still crackling in the air. Charlotte met some of her friends, Gaff's pharmaceuticals were in great demand and Chris and Billy seemed to be chatting to every Mod in London and beyond. Even some of the Glory Boys seemed friendly enough Chris thought, despite the disdain they had dished out at Wrexham and Chislehurst. Southend seemed like a magnet that had drawn them all together. All through the year they had been little pockets of Mods scattered across London and the Home Counties, meeting up at gigs here and there, but tonight it seemed to be falling into place. The Lyceum had been fantastic but it had been an experience they had to share with a load of other punters. Tonight was for the Mods only and for Chris it felt like home even though he had never even been near Canvey Island before.

Squire soon kicked things off onstage and the buzz that Chris felt inside him intensified. He was not sure if it was the pills, his mates, Charlotte or Southend that made him feel this way or maybe it was a combination of them all. The past ten days had been fucking nuts. A head-long rush through a cavalcade of music, sex, violence and very little sleep. It did not seem so long ago that he had measured his weeks out carefully between school on Monday and watching *Antiques Roadshow* with his Mum and Dad on a Sunday night. He had squeezed so much into this month already he wondered what lay ahead. The possibilities were endless. He was part of a scene that was growing so rapidly, he had great mates, he had a beautiful girlfriend... even the spectre of Dave's undoubted incarceration could not dampen his rising spirits. Tonight things seemed to be speeding by once again in a blur of beer, chemicals, frenzied chat and music. Back To Zero barely seemed to have taken to the stage then it was time for The Purple Hearts to stir up the crowd. Chris danced and shouted and felt the sweat drip from the roof. Every time he saw Charlotte he held her close and kissed her warm, red lips deeply but he could not be contained in one spot. As he moved around the hall he saw nothing but friendly faces. People he knew, people he had just met all shaking his hand or slapping him on the back.

Gaff and Billy grabbed him as he was about to drift past them in the heart of the crowd.

'You all right mate?' shouted Gaff over the din.

Chris only nodded and smiled broadly.

'This is what it's all about,' yelled Billy as he squeezed him on the shoulder.

They stood together for a bit and watched The Purple Hearts until they finished then they drifted over to the bar where Charlotte and her friends were standing.

'You're back, are you?' she said cheekily to Chris. 'Have you said hello to every one of the Mod masses?'

'I can't believe it,' said Chris wildly. 'What a night. What a fucking night.'

'Not too shabby mate, not too shabby,' sniggered Gaff. 'And lucrative too.'

'Pity Dave's missed it,' said Billy.

'He'd only be trying to start a fight,' said Charlotte.

'True,' Billy agreed, 'But maybe tonight would have been different?'

The silence amongst them was deafening. Chris felt a little guilty about having such a good time but it soon disappeared as the lights in the hall dimmed once again signifying that Secret Affair were about to take to the stage.

Chris was almost hopping with excitement and he squeezed Charlotte's hand until her knuckles went white.

'Are you coming down the front?'

'I've had enough sweaty geezers groping my arse for one week,' Charlotte said with a smile. 'On you go Chris, I'll wait for you here.'

He kissed her once again and dived into the crowd that were once again gravitating to the front of the stage.

'Hold up,' shouted Billy as he and Gaff followed behind him just as the band made their appearance.

Chris had never thought too deeply about much in his life. Heavy pondering on the nature of the universe was not big round his patch and he had always just accepted the way his family, his school days and his circle of friends had turned out without too much effort. Tonight he felt different though. As the band played and their soulful racket swept over him like a warm blanket he looked around. He could only hear the music – no talk, no background noise, not even his own breathing. Although he was just one part of the tightly-packed crowd he had never felt so unique yet so connected to something. He saw his mates dancing and holding on to each other, smiling ecstatically as the beat drove them on, and he saw Charlotte in the background with her beautiful cropped hair shining under the bar lights and her eyes twinkling furiously as she watched the band. Everything that mattered to him in life had truly come together since he first discovered Mod. It was the soundtrack to his life, it was his life. The bands were singing about things that happened to him and his mates, things that mattered. They weren't posh punks pleading poverty or pop wankers peddling unattainable disco dreams. The Mod lifestyle was a living, breathing thing. It was real and all the things that mattered to him stemmed from it. If other people did not like it they could all fuck off. All the greasers, all the punks, skins, bosses and snidey music journalists that wanted to see Mod dead and buried again would have a long wait. He looked behind him at the crowds who were in it with him. Hundreds of punters that felt the same as he did. Millions like us. This was going to last forever. How could it not?